North of Yesterday

North of Yesterday

OR
Flowers of Waz

Thomas McEvilley

A NOVEL

McPherson & Company

NORTH OF YESTERDAY

Copyright © 1987 by Thomas McEvilley.
All Rights Reserved.
Published by McPherson & Company, Publishers, Post Office Box 638, New Paltz, New York 12561. Publication of this book has been assisted by grants from the literature programs of the New York State Council on the Arts and the National Endowment for the Arts, a federal agency. Designed by Bruce R. McPherson. Typeset in Monotype Lasercomp Times New Roman. Manufactured in the United States of America.
FIRST EDITION.

1 2 5 7 9 10 8 6 4 2

Library of Congress Cataloging-in-Publication Data

McEvilley, Thomas, 1939–
   North of yesterday.

   I. Title.
PS3563.C3618N6   1987   813'.54   86-33250
ISBN 0-914232-86-X
ISBN 0-914232-85-1 (pbk.)

Those who sleep are workers, and share in the activities going on in the universe.

– Heraclitus

For Them

North of Yesterday

Spring was turning into summer. I stood where the waves crashed, waiting for Della in the late afternoon by the sea. Birds rested on the swelling crests, fluttered up from their closing grip, then rested again. The waves poured closer, the sun sank down, and the birds screeched on in their game of death.

And Della was no longer just late. She was not coming.

She had flown through the crack in the vase.

I crossed the highway in heavy traffic and headed for the slum as the overcast cleared and fire was added to heat. I pushed through Della's door as a train approached overhead, and ran up the stairs, brushing the dirty wall. Quickly I knocked but she did not answer, as I knew she wouldn't, and then it was too late to knock again — already the train was roaring like a mad beast, like an angel falling. Bracing myself I kicked the door hard behind the lock and it flew open with a crash. Through the window the train rushed away as I entered the still, empty room.

Plastic curtains hung lifeless in hot still air.

The bed was unslept in.

I walked around breathing with open mouth the quietness that smelled only vaguely like her. I touched girl's clothes on a chair, whispered her name, looked at the bureau drawers and thought of pulling them open and going through them. Then I lay down on the bed and waited, smoking.

Grey dusk came in with that suddenness that you cannot see and thickened like thrown powder in the air. Soon I was not waiting anymore but just lying quietly with the smoke rising over me in the stillness. Then I was asleep.

The veil of waters rippled. Pebbles of light flared down in the swollen dark. Far off Quintus danced slowly in the dark suspension. His beard floated out in the currents and his eyes looked wild and sad.

He danced like the waves that dance forever, lifting his old knees high and tossing his whitened head like the foam of the sea. I saw that he had no other way to tell me.

I awoke staring into darkness and knew at once that someone was creeping across the room toward the bed. As I sat up he lunge-ed for me with a roar of inarticulate brutality, his feet crashing on the wooden floor.

With shaking hands I dug in my pockets and lit a match. Yes, Della's bed, sweat-covered now, yes, her room. The match burned my fingers and fell. The roaring sound was getting more distant now as the train raced away, and I sat back in blackness and remembered the angry angel who rushed over, and that this was his message that needed no words.

The room grew silent and again I heard someone moving in the darkness. I stilled my breath to listen for his, but he stilled his too. Dimly I could see him in the chair by the door now, watching me. Then he moved somehow in a silent flow and lay stretched out on the floor, gazing lazily. The hairs on my neck and arms stood up.

I found a cigaret and lit it and smoked for a moment. Then I grew annoyed with myself, clumped across the room, and felt the empty chair in the dark.

I turned on the light and went through the drawers of the dresser, leaving things scattered where they fell.

Della, Della, my mind would not stop calling. But Della was gone.

I lay on her bed again and a despair of many darknesses rose in the bitter silence inside me. First the black smoke of anger, rising sweetly from lungs to brain, I put in place, then shuffled those brightest black needles that were jealousy or loss or sobbing hate, and over it all smoothed the silk square of blackness that was death.

It could be opened when it was needed.

Distantly the dark angel called goodbye.

I wakened more. No. Sank more deeply into sleep.

I

1

                      Quintus saw
this book   and it
                      Quintus sang
this song   and it
                    Quintus dreamed
this dream   and it
          said   said   said

O thou who playest the lyre of seven strings — camest to me with sunlight in golden hair (*golden hair*) — where the blossoms I had gathered in my lap lay bright as suns (*little suns*). Oh white my wrists (*and cold*) with many a scream (*Ah!*) you gathered to the hot still cave and the flowers falling falling. Now the laurel hates you, the slender palm leaf hates you, and all the flowers."

        (Zeus, of all things beginning
        Of all things gatherer
        Zeus, to you I bring
        This first flower of song)

    Then Quintus marched out, and he saw the sillies, Della and Wally, Harry and Mary, sliding in the snow, while the sun shone, shone some, up above, but did not melt, they did not melt.
    Leaned at the bus-stop but already it was dark for this, dear sir, is Egypt, where it's always dark (*this is the silly*) and the little shops (*no not me*) glow (*not the snow! Oh! poor Wally!*) because humped little helpers (*slid on his belly*) working forges (*down the longest hill*) feed feed feed the little suns. (*Poor Wally Walrus!*)

Quintus! What is this rod of life? Thou art too old, my man. Sit thee down and dream by the fire where the sun, poor little sun, tries to die, and always some bastard runs up and pumps on the bellows...

So yes, it is night at last and another day in Quintus's life is done. Hardly is his victuals eat but he hoists his feet by the side of the stony forge.

Sleep, old man...

But in a dream one comes with yellow hair (*yellow hair*) and Quintus, old rogue, is carried off in his burning arms and pitched squealing in a deep dark cave and he knows what's coming.

No, shining one! Bugger not Quintus Smyrnaeus, the Venerable, the Inditer of brave tomes... But too late. The bright shaft is out, gleams near, and old Quintus feels its raging thumps.

Feet stir. He lurches up. Ah, only a dream. The fire has singe-ed them too close. Now Quintus is tired but he cannot sleep. The whores of Egypt stir outside his door. In vain will he dream of the Lydian snows tonight.

Shuffling his feet, he mounts the stairs and sits at his desk to curse Euripides.

No, Sun-god, thanks from me, you thief. And damn Euripides who made you, too.

He rages at his books.

(*Poor Wally Walrus.*)

(*I bring you flowers, my book, for you alone. See, from hands still wet with dew, brash violets, and the crocus still unleaved. Lonely and meek in the late dark I scatter them on your pages.*)

*   *

Quintus believes that the flowers of Egypt are the loveliest in the world, the pale papyrus blooms. So rising early sets out for that river of rivers where they spill their seeds on the bank. (*See, the lovely ones, they tire, their little heads are drooping.*) Out of the quarter of honest craftsmen, whom he despises, skirts the edge of the greedy mart of the Jews, and gathering gown steers reefed through the arch of Nekko who sent the Phoenicians round the whole of Afric dark and twice stopping they would plant of the grainflower and harvest it, storing below stained sacks of yellow gold. And sail on. Keels cleft black water. Ships sped. And silent leaning on the rail at night they saw the black ones who burned the hills around, blossoms of flame in that garden two years long, and tire and lean like failing weeds and fall. And drunk with the smell of rabble through the broad square Caesar stood and Quintus stands (*the red, the yellow, blue*) amid brown bodies (hurry on, old foot) and dips at last a hand (*their little roots get tired*) into the stream.

> So Quintus sat there half a day
> And ate his bread and cheese away
> Forty years had weathered he
> But old he looked as seventy.

Around him, like the drifting snow in his dream as he shrewdly naps, the gatherers move in swift files, into the water and out, reaping stems of the waz. For this flower indeed and especially the lithesome stamens of same they do hold exceeding potent for the healing of scabs chancres cysts and the pus-filled nodules that adorn the skull, exceeding bland when boiled in murky water and drunk thereof the juice, exceeding stable the pithy core for the fixing of words thereon, and exceeding pleasurable the stem when slithered up the ass. Millennia indeed have these waters nurtured the amiable plant:

> "Some say six, but others mighty more,
> The learned Greek hath set his mind on four,"

or, as that insightful tongue has it, *delta,* which doth seem to hold the greater potency as guess for cause of the remarkable coincidence which the shape of that letter bears.

Hence, in the gathering dooms of gallanter days, they bade adieu the mad Phoenicians and many a night lying to in the breeze that striveth for the pole (for they recked not of the anchor and sleeping couched on the deep they knew not where but some say with gorilla women) and did plant of the grain flower and eat it.

And strewn on the sorrel banks the barks of the Greeks, who think they are royal for their father was Alexander but they eat the fish quick enough and stink of it the same. Now see, they put out, with skinny poles a-pushing and their nets.

Above, the stalls of the Jews.

The Roman, of course, we see not here, for he flounceth about in the richer part of town, and is probably still abed.

Now here's an old gent who's fallen asleep in the slime (and with his pecker out!) and if we slip closer, yes if we sneak nearer, if we careful enough climb over this here rock, perhaps, perhaps we may have a word with him.

> And dochmiac or epitrite
> Quintus gets his metres right.

But to return to the children.

Wally Walrus slid down the snowy hill and lay back laughing. The sun was sweet and not even too cold the snow on his back or the back of his neck. And when he looked up one came to him with sunlight in yellow hair. "Up you go, Wally. You'll catch cold," Della said. And she took him away to a deep dark cave and was all burning and bright.

> Now what happened, Wally,
> What'd you do
> Back in that alley
> Off our avenue?

> Gold flowers in her lap she
> Offered to you
> What'd you do, old Wally,
> What'd you do?

The snow was warm under my collar and she came running, took me by the hands and I jumped up, I couldn't see, something was so bright. "Wally," she whispered, "you'll catch cold," brushing the snow off
my neck with her
                      hands
                      and I

ran
    with her
              up the hill
                      (*hurry on, old foot*)
and this oldfellow was sleeping by the bus stop (*look, his —*)

                Wally took the flowers bright
                And gobbled them from appetite.

"No.
"I took her home and her mother was there with those tired eyes, and after dinner she came downstairs and saw us on the couch and said wearily, 'Oh, go ahead, I know how it is when you're young.' "

Took her in the deep dark cave
                      (*By the deep river an old man*
sleeps and does not see that night is closing down.)
and smelled
            (*It is Quintus.*)
                    with her
                            (*Darkness*)
                                    the blooms
(*will take him.*)
            of love.

(*I bring flowers for his feet, to warm them, the new flowers, moss-rope and clandestina, for he dreams of the snows of Lydia and his feet grow cold.*)

> Quintus Smyrnaeus, born of old
> Fourteen books of heroes told
> How Troy was sown with Trojan graves
> And Greeks went harvesting the waves

And when we went down in the ships, wind heeled, sun seethed and incandesced, oars foamed. We ventured south, then farther south, till one morning our pilot Mago said,

"Look. The day comes on the right."

But we were already looking, dropping the oars against their leather straps in silence.

Then Mago said, "Wait," and rushed off in the half-dark, bustling worriedly, and brought the bronze discs and the dial and hung them from a yardarm and gazed across them at the last fading stars, turning the pointer this way and that. But the captain collared him in a leap and dragged him to the rail and shouted, "Just look, damn you —. There it is."

And on the right, over the dark land that should already have been water, the bright one came striding. Bright blossoms our eyes as the gold of his flaming hair filled them.

But Mago fiddled with the bronze and pointed with the pointer and blinked, declaring:

"No.

"For either we are in the open sea, past the bottom of land,

"Or the ocean stream has turned round.

"Or the earth has fallen from its chain of gold.

"Or we are in a new universe. Under an unknown sun."

And with fear like a bad breakfast in our stomachs we looked away from his blinking face and gazed at the rushing water that carried us we knew not whither, and at the ragged and immeasurable land.

In the late afternoon the stench of the river rises, and even Quintus, that lover of farts, cannot abide it. Rousing himself he slaps the bugs from his face, stands stiffly (*look* —), and shakes out his trashy robe, mumbling a prayer.

Above, the stalls of the marketplace are silent. Getting dark along the Nile. Boats of Greek fishers pole in through opalescent dusk. Oars dip and flash.

Quintus rises, staggers on the rocks, then steps, a foot, one, two, into the warm, and, skirts pulled up, wades down along and leans, gathering the last pale blossoms. He disappears in the dark.

Soon, splashing back with the browny-gold stems glowing softly in the lap of his robe, he shoes up on the rocks and climbs the steps to the street.

> Hurry on, old foot, thou'st many a stone to smite,
> And now the whores of Egypt stir about.
> Quintus sings as foot slaps stone
> And hurries through the streets alone,
> Sings the reign of aging Jove,
> Before the smithies stilled above —
> The bellows wheeze, the coction moans,
> The furnace shitteth precious stones,
> Now goddesses young and mamillary
> A-rot with rambler's dysentery
> Don spangled veilings and drift down
> To loiter through the torch-lit town
> And Quintus pulls his pockets bare
> A-searching for the money there,
> A piece of ass, a piece of ass,
> He letteth fall the dainty waz,
> His eyes bug out, he's uncontrolled,
> Quintus, Quintus! aren't you old?

Only forty, he slobbers, I look older than I am. It often happens to men of high intellect — I'll call you Waz, my dear, my lovely waz-lily, my estimable one, my Cretan flower. . .

So Quintus would lie in the house of the spirit vendor, locked in the arms of the spirit vendor's daughter. . .

Ah, Quintus, what is this rod of life? Thy little sun hath set.

(Besmirch not Quintus, my book. My book, thou hast lied. I kiss thy mischievous page.)

So praying, the priest sang in the stern. Daylong desiring the moon and the lordly stars. Those rich ardornments of our lady, Night. To set right whom the savage day hath wounded. And plied the oars, into advancing dark.

In the late gnat light Quintus gets up from his table and goes to the window. Far off, to the South, he senses that older Thebes, briefly sees Hector shining from a royal tomb, Love-lies-a-bleeding, on the snow. Warmer than he is accustomed to, the air puffs in.
He thinks how it is when you are young.
You lie back laughing and one comes to you with sunlight in golden hair. But no — he shakes his head and thinks again. You walk to one who lies back laughing in warm snow and in that one's eyes you are sunlight in golden hair... Thou art the shining one, my love... His breath is shallow, old.
And in the dark cave you shine like cold fire. And the blossoms that she has gathered for you in the lap of her robe glow like suns. And you take them.
Quintus grows cold for a moment, and shivers. This air is warm, too warm. Petulantly he gazes upriver, over the ramshackle rooftops.
The river is backward. It should not flow north. How do we know that it is north anymore?
Because the sun, that gallant man, rises on the left and travels through the sky and setteth on the left. And that is south.
And so he shines for an instant in the dark cave of the world. And if we bring him blossoms, he devoureth them.
Childishly Quintus shuts the window and shuts his book and sits and with difficulty restrains himself.
Not tonight. Tonight I will not curse Euripides.

And that night, as we lay beneath the benches, uneasy in the grip of that current we did not know, a cry came from the watch, and there was fire over all the hills. And clambering to the rail we looked, and on

the land there were black things, like men, that ran among the flames and did not fear them, and snatching a handful of fire would plant it elsewhere in the grass, and shriek.
   And the guides called them Gorillas.

   Quintus stirs. What cry comes north from ancient Thebes, sped on the venomous current? He is uneasy in this land.

   We scrambled for Mago, and said he would feel the heat of this world he had brought us to, and cursed
(Quintus)
        the pharoah from the land that runs backward who
(turns)
           blazed in his gold array
                        (sighs)
and his snivelling hairless priests who made the maps
                                    (frowns in his
sleep)
     and
        (finally)
             milled
                 (dreams)
                         about the rail in great confusion till
(of the warm)
              *the captain's men with their whips had
driven us back*
                (and beautiful)
                        like dogs.
                                (snows
of Lydia.)

              (*I bring you flowers, my book.*)

[13]

2

To any travelling gentleman of keen eye who chanced to have commercial cares in Littletown, on the river Sparge, in the valley, and who, while descending the train on a certain mild summer Sunday nearer the end of the millennium than the beginning, whetted that keenness on the passersby, excising fool from fox and sheep from shearer, Della's broad unornamented face, making its way as if weary of being seen, among the ladies in the afternoon sun on the sidewalk, would have seemed — if indeed it seemed anything but unexceptional — mildly repulsive. There was little in it that bespoke the monarchy of man, still less the mesmerism of money.

No, not for her, with lineaments as right for whelk as wen, still more for wart than whelk, not hers to be a mother's joy, nor, promenading among grander beauties in the sunlight, to rouse a summer dream in passing hearts and set the step for ranks of amorous youths; hers rather — if the truth be known — to be the cause of occasional tempestuous weeping to the former, and, to the latter, an object at worst of insulting and sly derision, at best, and only when beheld by one not under the watchful eye of his fellows, of mildly curious and not unfriendly regard.

Know then that it was no surprise, even to the dim folk of Littletown (who had lived long and learned little), and let it be no surprise to you, when, in her seventeenth year, having excelled in school without pleasing anyone and thrown herself singlemindedly and unabashedly at the town scamp and hog without disappointing anyone, at last in inner and silent weepings crying herself cut down, devoured, and disgorged by the rotund and idiotic boy, who thus tendered up with a guileless cruelty the only evidence of wit that was ever demanded of his life, Della wearily devoted a timorous heart on the altars of the unknown world one mild midsummer Sunday afternoon by arriving unremarked at the railroad platform, ascending the train from which only commercial travelers and youths returning from wars ever descended and, tapping the last shutters tight, pulling to the last door, passed into the locked dark of the nunnery of her mind forever, riding silently and without looking out the window through sunny fields, vineyards, villages, and towns, into the great grey city, there to wander the streets with unfocused eyes for an uncertain number of weeks or months without sending word to her family — whom, indeed, she had quite forgotten — or receiving word from her lover — for whom she waited, writing many letters but mailing none — and gathering in, as fruit of her adventure, the following memories: spilled bowls and grey rain; chill sunlight waiting for her on some stone building; her reflection crying from a bus window; a lightswitch on the wall of a public toilet vanishing and reappearing as she blacked in and out; a man pressing on her, in a corner where she could not remember her name.

She was not meant for this world, that much one could say with sad certainty. In the waves of that dead sea locked in her breast there was regurgitating a language which, for all the good will in the world, no one awakened to the pulsebeat of terrestrial pleasures could understand.

Not that it was heavenly — no, indeed; though wise men have said that the doors of heaven lie open in the sea, and I believe them. Were the alphabet of the world embalmed in monostich, it yet would wash free, in the largiloquent waves. But, as with cleansing fire, others have doubted whether it produceth more than it destroys, and the prudent may well direct their actions by the words of the poet, who says,

>Fear and forebear to drink thereof by night —
>By night unwholesome, wholesome by daylight.

Perhaps.

And whether we should be wroth that Della was not so prudent, and should rail against the waves, and kick about, perhaps the sea shall show, when it casts old letters crawling on the shore, testing their unaccountable new life. . .

Autumn comes in the city. A windy hand reaches for the leaves. There is a time when all ways are darkened. A fume of sorrow trickles through the rooms. Then while the air grows sick, the sea is strongest. It wields recklessly, like a god of old, its vitreous attraction. It sweeps in invisible ranks through the cities and harvests its own. And at that stop-throat time, while the leaves were fleeing in diminished ninths through the fields, Della entered the kingdom of the sea. Her money gone, her purse left on a bench, her name having scurried off among dry leaves, riding a tidal floe, in off the sunny street, to a darkness where breath was burst and the last springs were coiled too tight, she walked among bubbling fissures and chambers of bedlamite eyes, chill sun screaming in rain, and sat at last in a quiet place, and swam down and down.

Her eyes clicked.

Had she been dreamed by some aquatic god? As a shape of white rheum, perhaps, floating free of the mother-of-pearl? The oyster-like body trembling beneath the zero-click of her eyes? The tortured and unshaped flesh where belt pressed, making waist? But even if Wally had dreamed her, still it was hard to remember her, what she was. For in the drowned universe of the breast-locked sea memory basks in pure being. Motion is a gleam deep in ice. Desire sleeps in a still palace at the heart of time. . .

Della opened a door and walked through a noise like rain. A vapory gold spread over the tanks; mouths sucked and popped. She appeared at the top of a ladder and into her clicking orbs refracted: a floor; walls; a little house! *Wally!*

Wally did not awaken as Della, naked and white, descended toward him, a drifting lost white breath in the toils of dream. Eternal balneation, that was life. Sun and rain, war and peace, empire and devastation, these fell like mere petals from a great bush of time which would never be bare. And beneath it Wally slept where worlds rained down.

Della crouched near him and looked: gentle curl of tusks beneath huge bewhiskered snout. Big, big brown purse of a body. And *flippers!* She gave in to his breathing and her thought stumbled to a halt. Only vague waves of feeling came, sometimes finished by a wordlet which washed up with a tiny splash at the end: . . . : *Big,* or . . . : *Cold.*

. . . : *Touch.*

She touched his smooth slick hair with one hand, leaning on him lightly. His breathing did not change. Slowly she crawled onto him, laid her fat whiteness across his back and embraced with open arms his cold fur. She clung to his breath and rode down through rainy ages in the early history of the brain. Sometimes she saw the fish in the other tanks. They looked nice. She slept and then, waking, squatted by the water's edge and splashed herself. She felt like him now, big, guarded by layers of blubber, slow and safe in their home by the sea. New waves, laying on the sand stray tails of half-forgotten language, broke on her deep-locked nerve shores —. . . :*Wally!* . . . : *Love me!* — like the mewing of sea-birds, lonely, and so far inside. She crawled onto him again, caressed him, pulled his snout. The great brown purse of his body staggered up, opening unbelieving eyes. Wally raised a flipper and dashed her across the wet floor to the wall, then rocked tentatively, half-awake.

Sometimes Wally remembered night a little. It was a halfway time, a swishing easy time, a watchman flashing desultory light. But sometimes, falling from evolutionary sleep in new forms, he was reborn in terror and uttered the newborn's . . . : *No.* Now dark something and a light came for him. And he was afraid.

He heard her hit the glass and flippered around to look. There was a white thing making a crooning sound. The white thing got closer. Then the white thing was sticking to Wally, making him nervous.

Flapping, he threw her against the wall again and lumbered around to look. Slowly he perceived the white thing lying on the floor and went for it. But every time Wally would move toward the white thing to punch it with his tusks, a dazed wave, breaking, would sit him down in forgetful silence till it was gone.

Oh then the slow dance began, the white thing sliding like an elusive memory around Wally, stroking him, crooning at him, Wally rising in panic from hot waves of strange feeling, turning always toward the white thing with his tusks, she loving the gentle curl of them, he tasting a foam of blood on them, she feeling love, new-winged and white, rise from the ashes of her heart, he feeling fear, a white gull lost from its mates, rise keening over the ruptured sea of his sleep, and scream away.

But finally, yes, that wordless and confusing message from which the worlds have sprung did stun him slowly. He toppled under an onslaught of dazing waves, rolled onto his back, and lay still, wheezing. With the tenderest and most possessive of touches Della climbed onto him and inched up his belly, through the hot storm of his breath, into the orbit of his enormous, uncomprehending eyes, and kissed the great white tusks. He was tame. She nestled her head on his fur and lay at peace.

But Wally felt waves crossing inside him. His teeth were near the white thing and he kept feeling . . . : *Snap,* and blood kept foaming in his jaws. Then Della would move and stroke him, stroke that upright and questioning limb whose function he could not remember, and a forgetful golden wave, like trumpets rising in sunlight over a sea of blood, would spread over all his inner shore. His jaw fell limp. Gradually something almost warmth, almost awareness, almost interest, arose in him. He felt a new wave, . . . : *Want,* spreading confusedly everywhere.

Wally rolled over on Della and looked around curiously. Where's my soft white thing? Flippering, he waddled around to look behind him, and there she was, lying still. . . . : *Want.* He prodded her with his tusks. She slid groggily away as he started to mount her from behind. He waddled and stopped; she slithered and stopped. They moved haltingly about the little floor.

Wally's breath was a shrill whine, like something screaming in the tank. He passed the limits of his annual activity and, from recesses of sensible instinct which he seldom used, . . . : *Stop* came splashing. He lay down and rolled on to his back, panting. The waves were mixing up inside him now, . . . : *Warm* becoming . . . : *Stop,*

[18]

. . . : *Want* crossing over into . . . : *Snap,* and, worst of all, . . . : *Cold* rising malignly above the breakers.

Wally closed around Della with his flippers and rolled over into the tank. The crying of the sea-birds turned to joy as, plucking the still, white blossom of his love, he bore it away to the undersea world.

The water was cold and it was hard to breathe, but in a moment Della forgot everything except that Wally was holding her tight. She was, after all, one of those from whom the air had been taken long ago. A last all conquering wave cast the mightiest of all words staggering on the shore.". . . : *More!*" Della screamed, her last breath thrashing the water into foam. ". . . : *More!*" Wally trumpeted till the aquarium rang and the watchman came running, centered them in his flashlight beam, and screamed. Della felt all tightness, all fear, dissolving at last as the sea-folk greeted their new princess gaily. She passed into a still greater darkness, as Wally roared his love in a coronation of quiring convulsions.

3

Tonight, my book, we clean house.

First let us get old Quintus out of here, that fumbler, that fool. "Get out, old jackass! Get the hell out. No more of your bullshit, Quintus."

He stalks out the door, robes gathered in stiff dignity, not looking back.

I sniff a stream of impurities flowing through this book already.

But enough of squalor! Tonight, oh book, we sing of heroes.

When they dredge a criminal's body up from the sea, it has not rotted. The teeth smile, cheeks are full and dimpled, lips lush and red. The eyes look right at you. Sure and you think he'll reach right out and grab you, with a cold hand, laughing.

Only fatter. They gain maybe ten pounds from sea water.

Oh, too bad, you say. They were skinny and cunning before, and now they're fat and gay.

True. But consider. The sea water has preserved them. We must be glad to have them at all, you know.

Once up, they roam around Littletown, steal and stray, stab and storm, lie around in jail. And at first we are glad to see them again. Slap them on the back and laugh. Then the blackjack crunches on the head, hidden needles flash out and creep under the skin. We feel the cold hands (they never get warm again) fumbling at our pockets.

Then: "My money's gone. How long can this go on? They're stabbing me! I can't put up with this!" And back they go again, plunk, splash, into the sea, out of the trunk of a rented car, pockets filled with heroin and a razor-blade taped behind the buckle of a belt.

Where do they learn these arts? Oh, from one another. Or they hear the songs that the sea shells sing, or the rolling anemone tells them, in the long winters they lie smiling on the sea floor, getting fat. And so they rise forever with the tides, come summer, come autumn, come spring, wild gifts that the wry sea throws with ironic fingers on the shore.

I saw one once in the Fifth Street jail, his hair fell over his eyes. Not even tried and already he longed for the sea, the great salt mother who would rock him a winter long while oh so oh oh oh so terribly terribly cold but can't hug yourself or clasp hands tight between thighs because dead. Then finally not so cold (you get used to anything) and the nice fish bump you and you smile. They bump you nicely over and head sunk in the mud you smile a year long. Then a storm faraway and a little wave and plop! you're up and it washes your eyes again clean and your ears the mud out and you hear the songs that the sea shells sing and tumble you know not whither, in the cold cold sea.

Oh blossoms of sadness! Little roots feeling at the convict bench, his hair like little petals over his eyes. . .

> And he sat there for half a day
> And ate his brain and heart away

but still no ticket. No ships today, old man, for the wind that bloweth north and west by Pleiades and Hyades, Great Hunter, and the Wain, hath not yet rounded the Cape of the Mad Phoenicians nor rides fast up Red Sea coast but sails lie limp in waiting, and he that bloweth madly south by south upriver blasteth strong by the Dog and the Pig and the Rat —.

But Quintus is gone, old shoulders brushing out the door.

Easy now, pretend you don't see him — there by the ticket office in the closed shipyard of Littletown, taptapping on the boarded window in the dusk — don't let him meet your eyes. Who is that waving from the back of a passing bus? Everywhere those old eyes flicker nervously, which we do not welcome.

And one night while we were fixing boat hulls under the dock, stirring hot tar on the sand, he ran by overhead, screaming of flowers in his broken tongue. We smiled when a girl's feet pattered after. Later he was dragged by a hard-eyed man through a beaded doorway, a drugged girl waiting.

And when they asked who it was changed beyond recognition in the trunk of his car only the grinning flowers of the cops' eyes heard him, only the bleeding flowers of their mouths...

    Now come on, Wally,
    What'd you do?
    Put her in the trunk of your car?
    Where did you go?

Outside the jailhouse window it begins to darken. Last light by the boarded ticket office. Grey gleams of opal boats upon still river. Poles flash, dip. By the creek, at the bottom of the ravine, the children are sleeping.

    Night will come now.
    Or is it almost morning?
    The air grows cold.

Now, you know the feeling. You're in the car, a chilly Sunday in November, sun bright and cold, riding around drinking beer. Wally, who's driving, pulls off the road at last light and you all walk to the overlook, feeling warm and high from the beer. Far below, the beach grows dark and stained, with the ocean sliding in, then out, then in, drawing you and making you quiet. From so high up it hardly looks like it's moving at all.

Then someone says, "Hey, that's the place Wally's car went over last summer, and Della was with him."

"Yeah," someone says, "how'd that happen, asshole? Was she sucking at your dong?" And you all laugh while he grins sort of sheepishly.

"Yeah, what'd you do to her, Wally? What'd you do?"

Then he starts getting pissed off and cuffs one of you. "Cut the shit, you guys." And you all jump him and wrestle him down and run back to the car laughing.

> Now whatsamatter Wally
> Wally don't cry
> Della's a-waitin'
> Where the sea birds fly
>
> Gold flowers in her lap she
> Offered to you
> What'd you do, old Wally
> What'd you do?

If a night comes we will skip it for now. Perhaps a crime has been committed.

Who knows?

That old man scratching at the police station door, what could he tell? And look — on the sunny bridge, in a speeding car's back window, grinning nervously — what does he know?

Really, of course, it's just Quintus. He wants to get back in the book, but doesn't know how. He can't just ask. He's too proud.

Besides, I'd say No.

Suddenly I look up from my desk.

A sound of lamentation grips my house. Low and changing moans rise through the laundry chute. I stick my head through the little door and listen.

Della has gone mad in the downstairs apartment, pulsing like a trapped bird, warbling a low choked song.

Is Wally dead?
Where does such grief arise from in woman?
Who has given it to her?

(Speedin' up over the bridge
Where the sea birds fly
You can tell, Wally,
Wally, don't cry)

4

When Vincent's business is good Waz sits in the back of the store and eats all morning. Little fish things, oysters, and shrimp that she doesn't scrape the trails of shit off of, impart a greasy luster to her lips. Then she lies in the courtyard corner, where sleep drips from the gold-soaked boughs and bursting tendrils, and sings songs that she has made up or the old man has made up for her. Vine blossoms ripen in the shade, hanging their clustering heads. She sings:

> *Flower of new wine*
> *Grow sweet upon my pillow*
> *Like the odor*
> *Of my beloved.*

Upstairs Quintus dreams fitfully in his locked room. Waking when the girl sings, he goes off his head, and chains of nameless sounds ring through the house.

Afternoons are too hot in the courtyard, and she sleeps on the pantry cot, beneath the counter, dreaming of the deep river and the flowers that float upon it. Sometimes these dreams are sad, for often the irksome tide grows hungry and opens a peevish mouth where a flower will pass and swallows it down. Then she mews, and her petals ingather in sleep. But sometimes, as she smiles and opens her body to the air, the raw and tameless breeze catches a blossom and it veers past the round gulping water mouth and escapes. Then the hungry place waits ravenously for the next, and if none comes it swirls away down deep with a splashing cry. Thus in the deep river live unsatisfied hungers, petulant griefs, and angers. Moving in restless eddies by the banks they mouth with their watery lips the brown legs of gatherers by the shore, whose uneasy feet stir in the mud while, above, lithe hands reap waz stems, lay in robe lap. . .

> *Flower of the river*
> *Lily of many names*
> *Float into the hands*
> *Of my beloved*

She wakes up streaming with sweat in the pantry hole.

But when Vincent's business is bad, by the third week she is afraid to go downstairs. She lolls in a sun-barred trance where the old man raves in daily degenerating tantrums. Behind the locked door their voices merge in a queer enchanted song.

> *Flower of the brain*
> *Bruised flower*
> *Tell me the name*
> *Of my beloved*

At noontime Vincent comes and rattles the knob, screaming, "Daughter, your mouth is fat, you gorge your holes and make no money," or, "You eat the shit of the shrimp, you eat the oyster." Late in the day, returning, he hurls himself at the door in a frenzy till his shoulders ache, then squats against the dirty wall, glaring.

"They don't need it anymore. They need only their whores. May the ass bloody them." Then, whispering, "Come out, you whore, I'll stuff your holes with lilacs."

As it grows late Quintus breaks lucid and talks to her for hours about cool places. They welter in unbearable heat on both sides of the door as the old man's voice peals through the house in the language that neither of them understands. She listens with half an ear, if at all.

Then goes out where Vincent sits baleful, waiting. The door opens; the night is beginning to get cool.

"You're late," Vincent says quietly. He walks in where the old man lies in a smelly heap. "Come, you goat. We will make a nosegay of lilies."

Dragging him by the beard, he enters a windowless room where a thick dusty gold descends from a little skylight. He throws the old man to the floor like a handful of rice. Bottles of many-colored glass, sealed with pale wax, he takes from a shelf.

"The art of the body is clumsy. But we sell what is at hand. All things have strings, and the vendor holds them. I can sell you what you do not want."

He sifts dry powders, green and gold, and Waz inhales them through a xanthic straw. The old man lies in the corner like a foolscap, or a broken musket, or a dented helm.

"The body has drains to throw off its stinking messes. But the spirit, ah, the spirit needs no holes. All things are made new on the dragonfly's wing."

He mashes cock's eyes into a russet grease. "It glides through the limbs of the elders beneath their palm trees. It pulls the strings of the young, too, and deceives them." The root of a blue lily is boiled in a yellow dog's blood. The old man stirs dryly, like a crumpled paper, or a wounded bird.

"But like the deep river the spirit too has threads, those knots most difficult to tie and untie. And when it thinks to laugh and dance upon the surface, always the abyss is casting up new forms.

"Desiring at last to escape from the veil of light, it rides with the dogs, floats with the birds, abludes with water into mist and color and rain, and finds no exit. It foams over walls, thinking to escape in thin air, but is bound to the earth. At last it crouches in the body pit, a captive, but furious and untamed, thing, and torments the flesh with impossible desires, the blind hands grasping at what they cannot hold. Later it whimpers for sleep, stuns the body with stupor, and lies like a dying animal in the darkness, eyes gleaming.

"Take off your clothes."

Slowly she strips off the veils, and the molten light creeps in a slow tide up her legs, drips in slow rapture from her arms as they rise with the husks. The old man's, and the young man's, eyes gleam as they stare through her at nothing. His voice is a whisper.

"The threads go in, the threads go out, and not even the vendor knows the face behind the veil, whose slow breath billows the winding threads forever.

"Lie down."

He pours grey fluid on a cloth and a hungry sharpness barely cloaked in lilac darts about the room, like a rat's nose sniffing eagerly under the table and in the corners. Waz wriggles and cries out as the fuming cloth caresses her.

"Behind the flower, behind the water, the threads run on. When the birds rise up at mid-day, crying strangely, as in pain, and holding to no straight course, the people in the street look up. . . Someone has pulled the threads tight. Then perhaps business is bad for a time. Patiently one works at the knot."

An alder leaf, rolled into a thin cylinder, he smears with the sputum of a black lamb drowned in spring water. Waz is making little movements, probably involuntary, her eyes out of focus. He pulls apart her legs and inserts the leafy tube, twisting it all the way in among the petals of the blossom there. He pops something into her rectum also, with his finger, while she twitches, then burns the leaf on a little stone crucible.

Rising quickly, he grabs Quintus by the hair — "Smell, old man," he cries, pushing the mumbling old head between her legs — "Smell the blossom of my nosegay!" The old one rises, reeling.

Waz walks with a confused bright look, her nipples hardening, her breath loud, to the door. "Go, my goddess," he whispers, wrapping her in a filmy veil, "my lily of pale dreams. Tie up the strings of his body. And untie the strings of his purse."

Flower of the waz
Mute flower
Speak to my lover
When he plucks you.

It is late when Vincent swings his feet over the side of the bed, sweeps his robe about him like a sail of wings, and stalks from the darkened house, rustling the beaded doorway. Only the late-roaming dogs see him hurry through the hot streets with head covered, slide beneath the arch of Nekko, and cross the great square to the water.

Cries come, as drunken wanderers pass through the arch of Nekko with flaring torches. Crouching by the wharf, he listens, then, leaping to the sand, he pulls a little boat into the water, climbs in, and poles upriver in the reedy dark. Stripping off his robe he strains naked against the current. The moon rises and glistens on his pushing arms as for hours the pole cuts the silvery surface. Little screams come from the water where it splashes in, squeals of pain or anger, but he ignores them. As the moon is falling he steers into the reeds. In the boat's path legs rise dripping and hang for a moment like question-marks in the air, beneath beating wings that have not yet caught hold.

When he puts in to shore dark figures rise at once and lumber toward him, impatient, suffering, gurgling like the hungry mouths of water. Hurriedly beaching the skiff, he falls upon them, laying to with the pole. Again and again he scatters them over the sand, but always they return and bear him down, struggling. Some flap upon him from behind with their dangling walk too slowly, covering his mouth with their dark garments. Others clumsily try to snatch away the pole. Fluttering in a group they foam over him like devouring waves. But soon he rises from the pile with the dark things on his back, throws them off with great strength, and pursues them over the dunes.

Wings flash at river's edge. Gone presences ripple over dune crests. Question-marks rise from the reeds. Starting this way and that, he sees that he is alone. Day opens its lavish hand, spilling out new coin, first grey, then gold. He lies down and sleeps by the water's edge. When he wakes, gold prodigally flung has soaked the dunes and run molten over the lapping wavelets. He plunges in and swims, feeling the current, gentle but unappeasably strong.

He guides the boat downriver as the current pulls, and strengthless lips of water, which he knows will devour him someday, slip whispering by the stern. He walks home in the late morning sunlight.

(Flower of the wave
Grey flower
Embrace my beloved
When you meet him.)

5

That day was a warm one, and the next. But they pass, and then autumn, which means little... Rumors of a cold wind in the North. A bird alights one day on the arch of Nekko, and behind the Jews' quarter a room is cleared, old books with wearisome Greek names are traded to the landlord or given to the children for their games. The floor is swept, and one or two old dreams float out in the airing. An old man's name is forgotten...

Not far, the river spills into the sea; the wind flies over the waves. The great ocean sees the seat of old Mago's pants as he falls down from ship-side ass-end first, lands weeping in the chuckling waves which have seen it all. Bronze disks and dials splash around him, curses from whiskery faces. Then it grows distant, still.

Yet something's wrong. For one thing, birds are scratching the screaming sea. There's trouble there. Now waves are walking to the screeching sky. It screeches and runs.

He leaps up. All nature locked within a wheeling globe! You turn the dials. And know the ways of the wandery wavery stars... He shakes his fist.

"Oh Sea-god, this was your trick. You should have turned round but you've never helped anyone. And that pleases you, I suppose, where you range with your asshole friend the wind." He wanders in the sunny breakers which foam in garlands of laughter over his head and shoulders.

"Laugh on, you bastards, I know this is what you want!

"For at last I understand the thoughts of the sea which murmurs its lies forever, and of the wandering winds which slink through nose and mouth like thieves and only an odor of their meaning remains, though courteous always you address them. The stars, they march aright, those grandees of the night. But you, Sea-god, and you damn winds, you never cared about anyone but are always eager to pull us down and laugh. Well, laugh while you can, fuckers, for you'll get no more sport of me, for I've lost my plates and dials which were all I cared about and you who never give anything back have swallowed them."

And cursing the sloppy slappy waves and the giggling wiggling winds he walks wet-ass from the water and will provide it no more pleasure, but a new land lies there, however huge and hateful and unknown, and, pointing himself forever toward its jungles and darknesses and dyings, he strides smartly on with the wind in his hair until the silent grassland surrounds him and the snickering of the bickering sea cannot be heard.

> *Flower of green grass*
> *Flower of green*
> *I was ten*
> *And he fourteen.*

And when autumn came I fell in love with the dark-haired girl who was new in school, but she was gone again by Christmas, leaving a faint odor of lilacs which woke me from dreams all winter, a vague and dangerous greyness which sniffed curiously under my bed and in the corners.

Such dark and flower-scented girls will move on, like mayors' daughters kidnapped by Gypsies and dreaming of rescue, to other towns where boys will die in silence and swear to tell her, with a note in the schoolyard or a nickle coke, then arrive one morning eager and scrubbed and sworn to find she's gone, it's too late, darkest emptiness hangs over her little desk.

When the snow fell I still had dreams of good fortune, reprieve: she came back, and I saved her. But finally the odor of dreamed lilacs faded into March, and that was the spring Della's kid brother almost drowned in Old Lady's Creek, which held my attention for a while. Della stopped coming out to the woods, but walked on the sidewalks with the other girls and tossed her mane of blonde curls happily. Her breasts were just beginning to show through her dress. I followed her through the halls at school and hung around her locker, though it was not near my own. Occasionally still I dreamed of the dark haired little girl, but gradually her image faded. I found one morning that I could no longer picture her face; only that grey and dangerous scent would sniff through an empty and dimly lighted room in my dreams. My thirteenth birthday came that summer, and I asked Della to go to the movies with me.

Now, the nights in our part of Littletown had always a peculiar sheen, mostly because the streetlamps had ancient writhing globes of golden glass. The new parts of town have clear ones, but that is not part of the story.

Shall I tell you that a part of my life hangs still in those rich gold globes? At least, I have never been able to remember that night except from the inside of one. Some memories of Della are perceived as if through imaginary senses; others, through some gangrenous fluid; still others are heard within a deliquescing vowel, a sound bloodless and hushed, an eternal, dying resonance... Over this night hangs an aureole of inhuman light.

She appears, silhouetted in the doorway of her parents' house, a princess drifting through a gleam of death from a castle which she should never have entered. Something swivels, or breaks, in my mind. She swims through the fevered glow of the streetlights beside me, slow and molten, as if moving in amber, or in an unhappy dream, or from a grave. Smiling, she disappears in cold blackness under boughs, a wet thing entering its dark home. But worst of all was the hysterical silver staccato of the movie, washing her face in white blankness that hardly breathed, a negative, wild and beautiful as that pale dead flashing on the screen.

We emerged into the peaceful darkness of the square, where blossomy winds ranged lost from an eternal summer. Her steps, and her breathing, were a nightmare from which I could not even wish to awaken. Suddenly I found that my skin was crawling with every kind of sensation, like scalding honey, like spurting razor slashes and raw screams — I found that she was touching me, and turning, and smiling, while a girl's voice from somewhere said, "I bet you can't guess what I'd like to do."

Dear friend, can you believe me when I say that I could not, could not if it had been the only offering of wit demanded of my life, have made an answer? Things swivelled, broke, leapt over, and spun, in my head. A cry like a block of ice solidified my throat. I merely turned and staggered on, and a secret word seemed to leap from the throne of heaven and flare around us but remain unspoken.

We entered the shade of rustling trees, and again, soft tentative fingers at my arm, like snail-kisses, or bee-stings, calling, insistent. Relentlessly I strode on to where the last light trailed off into bushy darkness, then turned, strangling under that childish gaze I had thought I knew, and whispered, like a drowning man, a soundless plea.

And she didn't hesitate, as I had feared she might, or pretend she didn't know what I meant, but smiled with her little girl's lips near mine, and whispered as in a dream, "I'd like to walk through the park and pick some flowers to give you."

I pull the bell-cord as rain splashes at the windows. A church steeple rings and I try to count the strokes but lose hold.

From the dark hedge the breeze drew a summoning crepitation.

What a torrent of odors on the breeze! What whispering of springtime, companion to ships! On the high mountain the buds are golden; in the valley, already green. Far off, sails belly; joyous hands guide the keel; oars slop. In a mountain fastness young men sit like gods and sip chilled jasmine tea. Weapons and gear lie on the warm snow around them. Whylome arms clash on the plain in nutty sweet hate. The spirit hastens and the blood grows bold.

Entering the grove we find the one whom we have sought. A woman suckles a starving beast beneath a tree. We raise him up and gold flows from his head. We raise her up and gold flows from her head.

Reaping the tender grain we store it below in purple bags, bend knee to earth, and set out with the oars. When the wind takes her we unfurl the spare sails and do women's work, winnowing gold grain blossoms on the deck. The ship ploughs on. The chaff flies over the waves. They shine in the great sun-palace around us. Slowly the blossoms sink, like heads of drowned children, to the gods and monsters below...

The keels creak like thunder as we sleep...

I step from the bus to the wet street and can't tell where I am.

Around me horsemen lunge with slack rein, confusing the cars. The festival of criminals is coming! Notices posted are as soon blasted down by weeping cops.

But these horses are not gun-shy, nor do their merry riders fall. Whence have they come? Whence springs such daring and such shamelessness?

Judges rush off like fools to consult old books. Is there a forgotten law? Is there something which has not been considered? Is it the millennium?

No. But those blossoms of sorrow that roll in the deep sea caves have waited too long to be plucked. For them no new suns rise, no seasons return, no appointed time lies ready in the book. Languishing long, they have called a holiday.

Dazed by clamor, I stand at the bus stop. Car lights flicker on the wet street. A steeple rings and I try to count them but lose hold. It is a dream, but whose? An old man lurches from the alley, beard shaking with raving, the smell of hamburgers tangled in his hair.

It grows dark. Tires hum on the slick wet surface.

On the bus, Vincent the Vendor sits on the long back seat, on his left arm, under the sleeve, eight stolen watches, their works carefully removed. His rhinestone eyes half-lidded.

Autumn passes.
Or is it almost morning?

(*Oh blossoms of sadness*)

The keels creak like thunder through our dream.

6

So not day passes, but night comes.
On the beaches the waves begin to sneak out their scummy treasures, the dead ones that couldn't last in the cold so secret and trying. Cars of boys blast by on the roads, their mufflers noisy-hot. Elsewhere also the bright ones begin their walks on the land, the sea, clicking on the lights like flowing gold, rumbling the engines.

The train of bright lords promenades across the sky.

By breakfast time they will be gone.

My book, we sit with blind eyes in the dark. You grow sick and I nurse you — your little mouths are gasping! — fear drips like dewy sweat before my eyes. And as I slump down to my desk, the moon, that nourisher of mushrooms, haunts my sleep.

> What of the night?
> The jolly stars are set
> And now the moon is getting all awake
> And laughing at the fellows with the net
> Who hunt him in their nutty sweet hate.

Moon sneaks onto a bus, disguised in a beggar's coat, and peeks out smiling. The gang goes down the wrong street with their net.

But oh! poor moon! the driver wants his fare. "Now what," says the moon, "is silver coin to me?" And they throw him off.

He floats into a church and is given a job in the steeple lighting the clock.

The stars in the sky go mad, crying in gold and thunder for their king.

Night ships go off course, and rueful captains realize what they have suspected all along, that the stars simply follow the moon and now are gone winging erratically around the heavens like bees asearch for honey.

In the sea the night fish gasp at the surface, lost from their proper depth.

The cult of the moon god is revived.

Mushrooms die.

Sleep comes, and out of sleep, dreams.

The world is in total blackness.

>   Tell it, ye queens of song.
>   What ships cross in the night?

When we got down by Fernando Poo, wind fell, an evil current fought the oars. We prayed for wind and the mad priest cursed the sky.

Each night drift back such way we day oar.

At last we turned up a tidal river which spread into a marshy lake and meandered a strange sea way. Soft beasts like huge marshmallows waddled by us, looking.

One morning the black guides pointed at the shore and screamed.

"Gorilla!" they shrieked. "Hair folk of hair skin. People of dark wood. God has befouled them."

And on the shore, scurrying beside us, were creatures who scooted like bugs, then leapt up and ran like men. And the guides said that these were the people of the wind. And that we had found his kingdom. And we could hear him laughing in the mountains.

Putting ashore we encircled and cut them down with the steel, their hairy coats dripping red. Two of the women we carried off and bound wailing to the deck. Wind far off in the mountains grumbled.

But those hairy women tore at their chains, and would not be still, and the guides shrieked that they were befouled, and so we flayed them, and tacked their skins to the masthead, then rowed around in the marshfields, while the priest sang in the stern.

> *"Wind of thunder*
> *Hear your women*
> *Pause in laughter*
> *On your mountain*
> *Wind of deep sigh*
> *Wail around them*
> *Hair breast wild eye*
> *White tooth women*
> *Screaming wind*
> *Scream and howl*
> *They're empty now*
> *Breast vests and cloaks*
> *Wear them devil*
> *Wear and spare us*
> *Dark land hair life*
> *Hair death hair wife*
> *Spare us Mago*
> *Two year*
> *Grain grow*
> *White god wind fall*
> *Grain and gold*
> *Wind*
> *Here are*
> *Your women*
> *Cold."*

A Greek tried it, one Eudoxus, a merchant man. Took dancing maids and drink for night drift. Wrecked off coast of Fernando Poo. There was a vow he'd made to Pharaoh:

Never never never never never shall cry of peacock fall the Red Sea wave from ship of mine nor ivory foot nor ivory hand nor ivory tooth heart toe belly nose nail ass lash liver lie long in foul den of Pharaoh slain but live that I have sailed long sailed rowed sailed for on Indy wave and dark man, but cry wave and howl dog, break wings Egypt bird priest lice lick lizard hole and stuff lime up, I'll sail down past Carthage isles like bird on wave or dancing girl and make my money and pay no gold-skin goddamn birdman's tax — like an honest man.

> And he sailed south for half a day
> And ate his wine and cheese away
> And danced at night and sailed around
> Until the sea god pulled him down.

For the wind blows not at Fernando Poo.

So with the gorilla skins drying at the masthead we labored downriver through the winding marsh and into a sea thick as jelly.

And while we slept on the sea swollen with mariners' tears, a second time the mad priest's cry awoke us, and the hills burned on the right. Weeping with fear, we fell like empty robes about the benches.

But that bard broke lucid with unmeetable pain-fire in his eyes and said that the bright ones were walking in their garden in the evening, having drunk their fill upon the snowy peaks.

But no. We saw no bright ones. These were black, as before, dark rushers. Screaming they ran in fire and their shape was like men.

And the guides glanced wisely toward those tortured ones whom god has befouled, and whispered of a glorious soldier for whom they made way with fire. He will come and burn the hair off of their skin. He will come and burn the skin off from the blood. Burning like rustling leaves of golden grain, they will fly in the wind, be sown like wandering seeds. For this they shriek.

And some climbed the masthead, drooling in their beards, and kissed the hairy skins that rotted there.

(*Oh barracoon*)

And so the dread land past which we labored in sunlight slipped back at night, while the priest prayed in the stern, that they pull us not down, like an offering of children.

(*in sweltering noon*)

And one night I dreamed of Mago, he of the charts, he of the brazen disks, the dials, that lover of stars and conversant of many winds...
But he was not among us.

(*they lean in thee
griefs hot and black*)

So in sleep drifts the strange land by, till dark it washes (*flowers*) you up (*where grow*).
It is a life you dreamed through.
Do the same flowers grow in this land, stranger? The violent ones, the golden bloody ones? Bloom in the dark head cave?
Yes. Sleep is of dreams...
The tongue stills, the nose snores on the page, the breath comes in slow scented floods... So *this* is sleep!
And when we wash up in the imponderable tide, wander like Mago in the darkening woods, seek a hairy woman of the trees, wild beasts whom suckle with bloody lips.
Or off the bridge, streaking like a gull, the rhinestone eyes of criminal gangs gone black, rolled century long in the murk of the deep sea caves, and still, dredged up, slapped back and rode away.
In the streets we let go the reins and gave our horse halves their heads.

Now I will tell you how sleep comes in the night: wild blossoms we had forgotten begin to shine again in the cave.

The bright one wakes and stretches his arms for the beloved.

With a little *biff*! two ships crash on the sea and drift down where the dreams of lost men roll, their bright heads dripping mud.

So this is sleep! So *this*! is *blessed*! *rest*! . . .

When we were kids, walking to Kilgore school, a wooden bridge spanned Old Lady's Crick and the gully. I remember Della, in the summer, wading there, dress hem wet and sticking to her knees. That's how I want her!

Oh, touch me, hold me, dream of Della, kiss me, let me feel your hard girl's chest on mine, and lie down by Old Lady's Crick to sleep.

These flowers blossom at the water's edge — (*silly Wally, Harry and Mary, Sally, Jenny, slid on his belly*) — and crashing through the bushes the bright one comes, shaking down sleep from his laughing hair.

Creek flows. Little hands gather blossoms. Little mouths of water gulp around their feet.

"We would pull you down, sweet ones, if we could."

Brown stems sink into deep river. . .

(*'Bout eight PM, dey locks up. Bimeby ol' Wally, de big 'un, he starts to stir.*)

>   Go down, go down! The phantom horse rides down,
>   The glorious soldier races through the hills,
>   In mountain fastness golden arms hang down,
>   Golden drink upon the warm snow spills.

My book, we sit with bright eyes in the dark, and hear the pageants of the night prepare.

Hear! Hear! You! Slumped by the oar bench, slouched by the glowing forge —. Whip up that slave! His arm grows slack at the bellows.

The sun will die.

And I must have my sun...

For sleep moveth not in tripping trochees, but in the dochmiac that surges, then in falling Ionics.
Ionic minore, call to me, O old one, you of springtime, you of death in battle...

> *Flower of the undertow*
> *Flower unseen*
> *There's me, and my love*
> *And the river between.*

(*Bimeby ol' Wally, he push up on one fleeper, he push up on de udder, and he set out sweemin'. Gurgle gurgle, sezee. Where my sof' white thing?*)

And here an old feller sleeps tight (*his*...)

7

He will not be parted from me, my book! I am jealous if he looks at another.

We ride on the subway. My book sits beside me, his head on my shoulder. Darkness crashes past.

I wake to the conductor shaking me. My book is gone! "Where is my book," I shout, "my book that was sitting beside me?"

Wrenching open the heavy doors I run through the cars.

"Where is my book?!"

I awaken — ah, only a dream. He lies on my desk undisturbed.

But look — my desk is by a high-windowed wall, great chandeliers above... Ahh, the deep strains! Oh, the haze of the candles! Whence this somber conductor, beating the stroke for the viols? Whence this satin on the walls, this velvet flaming on the bosom? In the eyes of these ladies there dances a praise of death, and their eyelids droop and their crinolines crackle dryly. Musicians sweating in dark suits pull madly at violins while the candles drip.

My book springs up and runs out on the floor. All night he dances with pretty girls and kisses their mouths. My head nods down to sleep, but I am so happy! My book is a crazy dancer!

I stir on the splintery deck while the priest sings over the sea.

> "Whom alone sleep does not hold
> (This is an old one, often told)
> Whether he be most or least
> Night casts down in umbrous gold
> Whether he be king or priest
> (This is an old one, often told)
> Night shall wrap in chains of gold."

Gradually, like the calming of an ocean, the street grew still and, turning from the bus-stop in the clear midnight of Littletown, I walked down a dark lane where companionable old trees rustled. In the golden glow of the streetlamp a little white house on a corner was unexpectedly familiar, and my heart gave a leap. It was Della's old house. Something from my dream, I thought, must have brought me here. I noticed with disbelief that some of the windows were broken over darkness. The house seemed unlived in. Here and there a filmy curtain from long ago reflected the moonlight. Some desperate or obstinate yearning stirred in me, to awaken her somehow into my world. I puffed at my cigaret a while, then stepped lightly to the porch.

I knocked and, after a moment, pushed the door lightly. It slid open as if it had been waiting for me. Again my heart leapt, this time from fear, but to close the door again I had to step inside and reach for it, and somehow, in a second, I found that I had closed it behind me. I stood smoking for a moment in the shadowy living room among the ghosts of earlier visits, breathing with mouth open in the stillness. What if somehow Della is asleep here, I found myself wondering, perhaps in her old room upstairs, white breast or snowy flank exposed forever to the dusty air, waiting forever for me?

I wandered among shadows, dusty chairs, broken glass, walked down the hall to a door and pushed it open. There was an ancient bed that looked empty at first — but on second look, as I tiptoed nearer, yes, there was Della's father, just as I remembered him, crumpled and pale, hardly to be seen against the glowing moonlit sheets. I tiptoed past him, as on earlier nights coming to her in the moonlight, and slid like a shadow through a doorway. Dust rose as I crept up the stairs, my heart beating fast. Would she be sleeping naked? Suppose I just woke her and wanted to talk? Would she be frightened?

Slowly I turned the knob of her darkened door.

A ray of moonlight lay resting on the rotting mattress and dripped onto the rusty sprung coils of the bedspring. I stepped closer, looking for that vague form that might take shape out of invisibility, but this time there was none. I lay on the ghostly bed in the suffocating smell of death, then, rising, pulled out the dresser drawers and let things lie where they fell. Why did it seem that she was here, so close that I could feel her?

Running downstairs I burst through the door and left it open, ran across the little lawn. I walked down the cool sidewalk smelling her in every breeze, aching for her with every breath. Soon I was in a part of town that I didn't remember, where a clear white light descended from towering streetlamps. An irrational certainty gripped me that she was in one of these houses, laughing softly from somebody else's bed. I could almost hear her calling me mockingly. I looked at a big house and felt: . . . : *Do*.

I slid across a wide lawn, up broad front steps, and through a door that opened easily, as if a doorman were gesturing me in. I was in a hall like an abandoned hotel, or one of those palaces where tourists come to see old royal portraits, but empty in the off-season. Quietly I went through the bedrooms. He was a sloppy smudge on the pillow, like a big thumbprint. She hardly showed at all, a dusty mirror only waiting to be wiped clean. Across the hall their children lay like tired insects, little mouths sucking, hair tousled on the pillows.

At the top of the stairs something stopped me, and I listened intently. Their breaths were surging around me, chugging through the air as in a little race. A speedy one would catch up with a slower and move steadily past. Concentrating, I found that I could follow three of them at once. Every ten or twelve times around they would all hit one beat together, then pull apart. When I tried to fit the fourth one in I lost hold.

Breaking through some bushes in the yard I went into the house next door and looked at the sleepers and practised on their breathings, then moved on.

I worked down that street and the next and many more. No door kept me out. Leaning over the beds, only inches from the sleepers' faces, or crouched in shadowy corners of their rooms, I became lost in the breathings. In the still houses they pulsed like living things. Over everything they rose, curled, and fell back, like waves.

The bodies lay stunned and serene, washed in the ocean of breathing. Some were piled on each other, some still in an empty space. Some burned like chemical ice or glowed like dull neon; others almost disappeared. It's surprising how many people look like they're not there when they're sleeping. Looking a second time, you find that, lost in the whorls of pillow and sheet, a face is waiting to be seen.

I went faster as I learned the ways of the inside and could do a house quickly. From the streets, or peeping in the windows, you can't tell a thing. In a big big house one little breath might rasp, frightened and thin, running and hiding through the empty rooms. You track it on the slow spoor of sound. Elsewhere at the very door you are assailed by a clamor of sighs. Some fight or hide, whine or grow frightened at another's approach. Some are tied in a knot between rooms.

Wandering among their beds, I wondered where they had gone, the people who lived in these empty heads that breath was keeping warm for their return. And, brooding over the tangled limbs with my own breath bated, after many many rooms — and she not yet there — I began to hear what they were saying.

They were singing of living dreams! These houses were alive with dreams!

Each head was a door to another world, and messages came back in the breath. The rooms began to get hot. Lost in the choir of dreamers, I saw how some furious ones fought with mad dreams, their breath growing strangled and tense; how others, almost pulled loose, went seeking through many passing worlds, perhaps even then washing up on some foreign shore.

Finally the various rooms began to burn with uncomfortable fire, and faces I didn't know, and some that I did, and other things, appeared in the flames. I was burning in the fire of their dreams!

All the worlds are in the fire, and the sleeping people burn in it. Outside it doesn't even show on the windows. My head reeled as I rushed through the dreaming flames.

At last, near dawn, I sat down on a curbstone and cursed Della. The bitch, the whore. Only her bed was empty.

Where had she awakened?

> (This is an old one, often told—
> Night casts down in umbrous gold)

At last the haze of the candles grows oppressive in the room. The mad violinists put down their bows and look sheepishly at one another.

Thinking the dance is over, I wake up at my desk. The room is dark and quiet and a breeze sweeps through with only a hint of the faroff steamy jungles. I stretch for a moment in happy satisfaction.

But listen — there is a riot of soprano and falsetto laughter on the breeze. My room fills full of their white arms and tinkling voices. Fingers ripple through my hair.

So the dance is not over! Nay, rather, hardly begun! Some king has died in the night, spilling upon us the greater meaning of his blood, and now we silly ones must dance in the cosmic shadow.

They take me by the fingers and hair and fly off with me over the treetops, to join hands in a mountain ring.

> Whether he be king or priest
> (This is an old one, often told)
> Night shall wrap in chains of gold.

(But one there is whom sweet sleep holdeth not but rising in darkness he donneth the skin of a beast and walketh north by sea-swell)

High among dark woods I dance with those cold night blossoms and hold them tight. I kiss the locks like petals down their cheeks. At last until their eyes go glazed, my girls.

They lie back on the grass and a stiff darkness fills them. I too feel it and sink down. Under the shrilling of the pipes a stranger walks among the torches.

We see that he is the most beautiful of us all.

There is a flower he has put in the wine, and looking down at the cups we see it now, the purple and greeny bits that float about. It has loosened our limbs and made us unsure who we are.

Oh, but an incomparable sweetness it lends to the wine! Staggering up I drink again and dash the cup down and sing. It is more than wine that rages in me — I dance like a god and fall into the stranger's arms — I stoop to the maidens on the ground and squeeze their breasts and kiss their stunned still mouths.

It is not sleep that comes, but blackness. We are like the dead and lie back with blood on our lips.

From high up the mountain the pure ones come, the white and gold. I see them but dimly and cannot move. With stately ways they move among us and are at ease.

They take the red-faced stranger by the feet. They raise him up and gold spills from his head. It flows among us and we are nurtured and sleep.

(*The keels creak like thunder through our dream*)

It grows late. The wind slackens, then rises and moans through the tossing treetops. Look —

Into the mountain clearing where dancers lie bathed in moonlight, old Mago races, jaw shaking, raving at the blue sea below. He preaches to the winds. "Even so, behold, you air high and fierce, the brash violet doth survive, and crocus coy, for they are young oh bold young go-ers of voyages." His musty breath fondles the petals. "Their little roots (*their little roots !*) flag less than lilacs' which lingering not long in the lowlands tire and gasp and fall into the hands of girls who wait, so. . . That gasping fall. . .!" His eye catches sight of the sea far below and he flings an arm at it. "But you, oh spilled-about-our-feet, vile sea where forever the rootless wind-flower toils. Never shall he grab hold, never be sighed on by girls and bosom-warmed, but under rushing water be carried forever through new worlds unknown. And he shall be called a blossom of sadness, for living beneath the cold waves." Peeping shrewdly, he recognizes the waves, and calls their names. "I see you now, Chryspalens — and The Shore — and Gripper-tight! Ha! There's Needle, and that's Red Wolf, and The Lie." Forehead wrinkled with concentration, he listens to a flower. "The darling! Its petals weaken! It is in pain! Listen!" Crouching, he cocks an ear toward the ground. Below, a thousand tiny mouths are round and gasping. But the old earth is hard. A grain of sand rolls up and blocks a little mouth. Then another. *Another*! He leaps up, crying with pain. "Take your sport, you wretches!" And is lost among moon-glints on wind-beaten stone, while the breath of the sleepers fills the grove.

> (*and meeteth that bold one who weareth the skin of a pard and goeth his way and lighteth the hut of that old one and cries not Wake you but stands and the old one inquireth for the seeking of beasts of burthen by night*)

Waking at night on the splintery deck, I go to the rail and gaze at the sea in helpless bafflement. At last I realize that it is absolutely immeasurable.

Bronze disks could not help us. Mago could not help us. No god could help us.

The waves laugh at them all.

I squat on the bowl, then throw my shit over — "Take this my gold, O sea" — and drift back to sleep, while the song of the priest floats over the splashing waves.

> "Sea-swine, come wallow,
> Sea-raven, a word,
> Sea-willow, sea-swallow,
> Come tree, come bird,
>
> Sea-spider, come weave,
> Let the sea-slug mourn,
> Inweave, outweave,
> Sea-weary, sea-worn."

(but grumbleth not long and donning the flowing purple goeth his way as bidden and the old one straighteneth his course and the twain pass on and that dark one reacheth the tent of that brilliant one, that lordly clever one, and rouseth him and the twain pass on)

When I got home late from the dance there was someone huddled on my doorstep in the dark. He woke at the sound of the carriage wheels and held out a message, then followed me upstairs, dragging something.

I saw by drawing room light that it was a note from Quintus. He had sent me, it said, a case of very warm beer, a small book bound in velvet, and three flowers: a yellow, a not-quite-red, and a definitely-not-blue. "Please forgive, me," he wrote. "I was a boor."

Well, he certainly had been a boor... But perhaps I shouldn't have blamed him for everything. And often, since he had gone, I seemed to see his old eyes flickering nervously.

I rummaged through the package and sipped on a bottle of the beer. Really, I should not have made decisions about the book at that hour. Finally I said, "Oh, tell him alright," gave the messenger a bottle of the beer, and sent him on his way.

Oh barracoon!

Hardly had he closed the street door when I drifted off to sleep, like a flower on the river floating into waiting hands.

(and at length are come to where that young slayer lies whose hands lie wet with blood and cry Wake you why all night sleepest thou and that young hero when he rises swirls out a tawny skin and behind his head the head of the lion lies its dead mouth streaked with blood)

But twice later I wake in the lone and vision-tending dark and lie silent in the grip of the waves. Long after, and still I dream of that dark little girl — the mayor's daughter — and walk past her little

white house in the early dusk
(and finally when the tide)
      walking my bike
           (changes sink down)
and look
   (this little turd)
       to see if it bears any sign
(where dead men sleep and their eyes)
         of the funny
             (are bright)
little painful
    (and rhinestone glittery)
          and soft little
(glittery jittery)
    kiss
      (as Vincent the vendor's.)
I never gave her.

8

That winter was one long night for Quintus. Or rather, that night winter came early for Quintus. Or rather, he caught the ague. His mouth shrieked while his brain burned. Daylong he cried for blankets in the windowless room till Vincent would hurl back the lock-bolt in a rage, storm in, and beat him senseless.

"What's the name of this hotel? Taverner, instruct my relations to change my residence! Fetch me a blanket, you idle boy!" Crazed at being addressed as clerk or boy, Vincent would strike with redoubled fury till the old mouth was bloody and still.

Thus Quintus slept badly. And this was the winter he became convinced that dreams are memories. For example: he woke in a field of velvet flowers. The sun was black, but the flowers, red and orange, glowed, when the black light touched them, with unbearable splendor. A blue cloud puffed out of the blossoms and surrounded him sweetly. He swooned back to his breath rasping in darkness and felt a fool to have forgotten the garden for so long. Lying in the room which smelled of his odors and which from time to time the sun, rolling behind the old boards and through the cracks, would people with inscrutable parades, he set this dream against the recurring and unpleasant one of sun-rape, and came to feel that Euripides had dealt fairly with him after all.

Conversely, in these rambling meditations, he found himself

believing that memories are dreams, that is, that they are not real. "If memory is real," he would argue, "how is it that I remember the shipwrecks, Greeks strewn on the unharvestable waves, dull Menelaos late returning. Oh and great Hector's funeral — the pipes went mad — his head burst like petals in the flames and honey poured out." Then he would hear the girl singing in the pantry-hole below,

> *Flower of the mountain*
> *Fall on the grave*
> *Of my loved one*
> *Like a summer snow,*

and only by clinging obstinately to the facts did he keep himself from believing these deceitful dreams.

Suddenly, finding himself cold, he would shriek, "Blankets, you filthy boy," and wait with wild eyes for the door to burst open, and the fists.

All that long night Vincent's business stayed bad. Rarely did the robed figures with covered heads arrive, follow him into the room of unguents and feathers, and hear his voice ring out in brief mastery. Mostly they came for Waz, spilling small coin on the counter. Taking the money, Vincent would close himself in his room, and they would seek her through the house, taking her on the pantry hole cot, the kitchen floor, in the courtyard — sometimes in the sun-speckled dark where the old man rattled and raved beside them, not recognizing what they were doing, as she herself did not. The aphrodisiacs had a cumulative effect, and Vincent would find her sitting with glazed eyes, wetting her pants with unprovoked juices.

Slipping in while Quintus rattled with delirium, Vincent questioned him in the demotic tongue about his friends and relations, took down names and addresses, confiscated his notebook and ransacked it for more. To each he wrote in desperate hope of ransom: "If you want your old goat back," or "Your grampa is a stuffed lizard sure if you don't" — then instructions, endless in their subtlety and indirection, for the sending of ransom money, the recovery. He paid small boys to roam the Greek quarter saying, "Do you know an old man like this?" — then make a goofy face.

Above all he strove with the knot, that the birds might rise again at his command. Poling his boat in the pre-dawn dark to the upriver dunes he found no flapping spirits waiting to be mastered. Some other had wrestled them away.

Lord of the sun
Lord of the tightening bow
Strengthen me
For you also are of song

Meanwhile, in Littletown, the moon is replaced by an artificial one, hung from towers, that saps the public generators, stalling the trains and trolleys.

In the sea, that dark place which I worship and where I know I will die, changes (what else?) take place. Dim shapes emerge from the waves and scamper over the sand slopes to the highway, on their way to the party. They lope down the left lane wickedly, their brown potato eyes glowing dully in advancing headlights, causing wrecks.

So praying, set out on the night-time portion of our adventure.

At el stations and subways, they grunt at the ticket booths in perplexity, pawing at money. When the trains come they hang from the straps as from branches, perch on the backs of seats, or pad down the aisles with heads lolling.

Now, oh girl of the shining breasts, be with us
And let a clever man be at my side.

I sleep well for several hours during this time, for as the messenger left I ate the almost-red flower that Quintus had sent, washing it down with a draught of warm beer, and it was the poppy, drowsy-rich. I leafed idly through Quintus's book for a moment, then floated away on the ocean of sleep as the drug flowed like a warm hemmorhage up from the base of my skull.

We ran like ravening dogs, but silent too.
So praying went out, lay among corpses, hid.

I dream of sleep and, as my breath grows slower, that dreamed sleeper dreams of sleep in turn, and so on till ten thousand dreaming selves wash up in different worlds.

From the corpseyard that clever man arose, slipped
the blade greased black beneath the chin, head still
speaking fell to earth and rolled.

The selves split into gangs and dream beneath creaking benches on the night-ships. They roam black jungles where captains gather in robes of beasts. Hairy women crush them to their chests. Rooms darken to caves. Night-flowers hiss blue fog. I raise my head from the pillow, my mouth streaked with blood. From high up the mountain a bright slayer comes, sunlight in golden hair. Face in the mud, I lie among singing shells and smiling bandits, my flippers swaying in the currents.

For the dark land changes all things save only the dark
shape of its law.

A shivering nerve wakes me. It is still — or again? — dark. At once I have an impulse to go out. Buttoning my coat I pull the door to softly and head for the bus-stop.

And so went on where camp lay to the North
Of Thracian Rhesus, king of whitest steeds
Among the sleepers lay the Thracian king
Among them slept king Rhesus by his steeds

The warm sweet night refreshes me at once — a field for balmy lovelings and lissome lovertines. The trolley comes chugging up, stalling every few yards, zapped by the moon. I ride over streets that shine with a sad fluorescence, and watch the couples strolling by the Sparge.

> *"Untie the horses," that fair slayer said,*
> *"Or I will kill or you," and cries rose up*
> *And groans where steely blade would touch the flesh*
> *Of dreamers dozing round those whitest steeds*

This is not my world, the undersea, where things happen at random and all forms are ground back into the featureless and primal sand; this is the dark shore, where nightmare and rumor rule with ironfisted logic and invincible law.

> *But bold Hippokoon quick sat upright*
> *And recognized his friends' old bodies bare*
> *Of armor save where red blood wound about*
> *Them, sad protection, Oh! He sat and wept*
> *And heeded not the trumpets, or Lord Silverbow,*

Soon the bus enters a sea-side area of jingling girls and wandering punks. They stand in the salt spray on the boardwalk with brilliant eyes, robins' eggs with rhinestones glued in the middle, a sparking deep within like wires torn loose or faroff summer thunder in their heads.

> *for dark dark lay his friends in death around him,*
> *and silent the ghostly steeds they rode away on,*

Each, in the pride of this light that does not dim, glows stilly, longeval and omnipotent emperor of the stars. Their bright mournful girls glare and flare like exotic birds in steamy cages.

I pull the bell-cord as the bus stalls to a stop.

> *with a gallant fling of the head, with a merry cry, with*
> *proud robes gleaming, hooves a-stamping, ghosts a-*
> *squeaking, scurrying overland, over the windy plain,*
> *into the flat sea whence, they say, there is no return.*

I leap from the bus in front of the Oceanside Dance Hall. There is a rank sweet scent with the flash of a blade behind it, from the sea and the garbage-strewn beach. I walk toward the door where the juke-box is playing their song.

    Oh where will you go, my boy-o
    And what are you going to do?
    Your blood runs quick as water
    And your eyes are scaredy blue.

    You've got to run, my darling,
    For you killed me with a sword
    You put me in your car trunk
    And you made my body cold

    They'll take you to the station
    And they'll make you cry
    And they'll speed you down the highway
    Where the sea-birds fly

    They'll pop you out a winder
    (Got a 'lectric button there)
    And you'll splash down under water
    And won't nobody care

    You'll hear the songs the shells sing
    And you'll tumble every way
    A little ocean flower
    In a sad sea bouquet.

9

Sea wrack on saxifrage tells it.
 By Mt. Pangaeus, Smyrna where Asian Sardis lurks behind, cruising past Rhodes and Cos, Cappadocia, Cilicia; round behind Cyprus and down the long flat stretch; Ras Shamra of many tongues, where the learned Greek lies drunk in the zone of Baal; Arados, where brown boys on the wharves grow idle and lean on crates and gaze at the sea; Byblos, where bald women shriek; the twin cities, and betwixt them Sarepta, where a youthful Mago waves from the dock, a smiling slob, and sheets of his lesson book fly out in the breeze; Sigmona, Magdiël, and Dora Dor; at last by the mouth of the mother of rivers, cargo from Pelusium, where ships lie to with limp sails waiting for wind from the Lost Phoenicians while the cries of peacocks and the odors of the Indian spices they feed on splash on the waves; then near Iamnia or Azotus meet the eastward flowing current from its cruder homes, Bocchus's or Cyrene's, where lie the dead Philaeni; Katabathmos, the descent into darkness; and meeting they squeeze and squirt back, shunt through Messana and Gaulic straits, rushing past Day Watch and far Tartessus, where the ships waddle low in the water from weight of gold; or north to the Faroes and a land of ice. Then night falls on it all. Only eyes gleam here and there. Beasts bump in the dark on the plain by the snow-warm mountains. Heads of lost babies gleam on the ocean floor. The many figures are washed in the burning worlds. The strings are tight.

Down long sand shores I gather in a double-breasted suit, stuffing the shells and slimy sea blooms in my sack. Stopping, I look at the waves, as wetness passes from my shoes into my socks.

When will I dive beneath them?

Or when will they come for me?

A pile of sticks trembles, shaken by unwarranted cold. Quintus twists in his filthy rags like a broken bird. Oily brown hands pierce him and pour in the mummy fluid. He knows he cannot fight this last mortifying anguish. Now his blood is gone and he lies like an empty sack on the cruel and mercenary sand.

He wakes and his eyeballs, bulging and bright, make darting forays around the room. For once he hears his breath as it must sound to others: pained, irascible, thin. Desire is not in it.

He feels reborn, but into extremest old age. He cannot remember where home is, or if he has always been here. Only, disconnected images roll like spilled beads across some dusty floor in his mind. . . Sunlight gleams in yellow leaves or hair. Sails belly on ships. Gulls wheel and cry over wharves. Dust is blown from old books. Then the darkness out of which he wakes now weeping quietly for shame. Crying and fighting. The shrieks of old age come round at last to imbecile stupidity. A long night wallowing in apish grease.

Slowly he abandons his past. He remembers the goddess who rises in foaming fire from the sweet sea, gold flowing from her flower-strewn lap. She has turned her back on him now. She is for the young. That cold goddess, who clutches you to her breast and it is ice, who drifts like a fume of smoke through her dark castle, phantom hounds at her heels — henceforth, he knows, to that one he belongs. . .

Later, as afternoon riots into heat, he is clutched in its fist of sweat and lapses back into idiot sleep. Doors open but it is never her door. A blinding light wakes him. Steps approach and a loud breath leans close.

"Where are they, old man," Vincent whispers, "where are those names living?" With a little cry he grabs Quintus and shakes him like a bag of rice. "Where is Walrus," he shouts, his eyes gleaming, his breath so close that Quintus takes some warmth from it. "There *is* no Walrus! Where is Walrus and the other names living?"

When he is gone, Quintus lies back like a dead man and sobs. Who *is* this devil? What foolishness has he said to him in delirium? What mad dreams is he to be held accountable for?

Vincent paces wildly in the room of flowers. Rolls of his books he hurls this way and that. Flinging back the door he floats like a storm cloud through the house and finds the girl singing.

"Come, my rosary," he whispers, tugging the lute from her hands, "come, pure one, sister to lilies," lightly taking her fingers. "We have a new plan — I will make you more beautiful than all the Pharaohs' daughters. . ."

She follows, leaving a wet place on the cot.

Flower of my lover
Which stream has captured you?
Why do you float alone
On the hungry river?

My hand, searching my pocket, closed on the second of Quintus's flowers and dropped it on the bar, where the pure and nauseating not-blue gleamed dully among the quarters and dimes. I pulled off the petals and washed them down with gulps of raw whiskey.

In sweltering noon

Around me the dancers swirled slowly, a curious barren rapture lighting their faces. I slipped from my seat and slid among them like a pale wave. A net of silver entangled me with unutterable sweetness. The Oceanside Dance Hall filled with water.

Dimly I saw a figure enthroned in a dusky cave, gleaming in ivory and fur. A sea-globe gonged a greeting out of time. Sea-trumpets groaned, sea-urchins plucked their lyres. Dead boys sat with slowly flowing hair on giant clamshells round a dancing fish and drank sweet lemon drinks from shells which little sea-horses bumped in with soft noses and everybody laughed.

I quaffed one off and dashed the cup down and danced — but no — even as I tried to join them they faded. I danced alone among alluvia of oceans cascaded by burned-out stars. And through me as through all forms I felt the old sea-tug pulling, shattering and reuniting the bonds of thought in a weave forever new. The cauldron of nature was transfiguring me through the elements! Hippoes lunge-ed and the jungle rioted around me. I danced in the lap of the earth, in the navel of the mother, flying in a ray of jungle sunlight, a devil-monkey leaping from the branches.

"Cut that shit, jack," someone shouted, "not in here you don't." But whatever it was I couldn't stop doing it. I was having some kind of fit on the dance-floor — fell over a table bringing glasses and ice cubes down with me and lay there, twitching. Vomit rose warmly into my mouth and my head slumped into blackness.

From somewhere came a gust of cold trumpets, and unexpectedly death rose before me, somber and full, a bronze door closing forever on a windy corridor. I was on the bus — figures were bumping in the darkened aisle — packages were being pulled from shelves — someone was pulling the bell-cord and someone else was calling goodbye and someone else was weeping. People were streaming out through the narrow doors and following them I descended into a confused darkness where it seemed that I wandered for hours or centuries through lives not mine. After ages I found myself lying on the sand beneath the boardwalk. The dancehall by the sea was dark and still. My head ached and stank like burnt wiring. Clutching my collar about my throat I walked out onto the beach, shaking with cold, vomit smeared in my clothing and hair. It was purest and deepest night — as if all other things were dead and night alone was tending the vision of life through timeless time. Nets of starlight fell smoothly through the tranquil air. I could barely see dim figures which hastened toward the wheeze and gasp of the sea. At one moment they would seem old piles of storm-stricken wharves, lapped by the phantom tongues of insubstantial seas, then would flutter and scream like birds, knifing the silence of the ashy air.

A sad thing it is when maidens must go a weeping journey before they have known the rite of love that crops its bleeding flower! They were seeking those lost ones who are eaten by the silent children of the stainless deep, whom some unreasonable passion doomed there, some loss or unconscionable need or gallant dream. Walking into the waves with wet gowns they begged for the treacherous tug of the undertowing tide to pull them to the caverns where their ruined loves waited, where in the rank wet dark among tangles of limbs once bright the chattering children of the untaintable deep laid bare with kisses of tiny teeth their secret inmost bones. At last they slunk beneath the waves, last breath bubbling up in careless laughter or sliding in dreamy song along the foam. I stood alone in moonlight and wavesound, the water lapping at my feet. Like quenchless engines the formless foaming bluffs churned tirelessly in.

I saw that the sea does not deceive. Each one finds in it what he most desires and most dreads. Something like hatred or fear arose in me. My spine trembled with some new autonomy and my brain felt like a blown fuse. As I climbed the stairs and headed for the street I cursed Quintus, the bastard, the fucker. Was he trying to kill me? I never should have let him back in the book. Finding a bus-stop I sat on the bench, stuffed my hands in my pockets, and tried to sleep.

But it was no use. My head hurt too badly yet wouldn't stop thinking. Something didn't add up. The more I thought about it, the less likely it seemed that Quintus had sent this gift. Not that he was too virtuous, but that he was too stupid. I wondered if he were in trouble. Some more dangerous and brilliant mind than his must have devised this adventure for me. I even wondered if this anonymous antagonist knew what order I would take them in, making the first one pleasant so that even after the shock of the second I would still be tempted to take the third.

Uneasily I realized at that moment that the third flower did already interest me. I took it out and studied it. It was wrinkled and yellow and small. But no. Looking more closely, and with an increasingly practised eye, I saw that it was in fact a shade of definitely-not-yellow, rather, a kind of pale saffron with a dull or hidden hysteria inside it. Not sunlight but a savage electricity waited there. As I gazed into the round sex-center of the flower I could see a veiled but still glittering gaze watching me from behind the dust and seeds. Gently I covered it and put it back in my pocket.

Looking around, I realized why no bus was coming. They had

the moon up, and strangely it lit the air with a frosty glow. It was at the full and much too bright. It would be like them to keep it always full. Also, it was smooth and featureless and lacked something of the old moon in that. There would be no trolleys that night. They would start again at new moon. If there was one.

    Hands in my pockets I set out walking under the maleficent glare of the metal moon. And the wind, that lonely comrade, sang a sad song in my ear.

There's a bus to Racine or Savoy,
To Egypt, even to Troy.
But where you are going, my friend,
That's the empty bus marked The End.

There's no crowd for that country of dark
Without citizen, monarch, or clerk,
Where the loneliest wanderers drift
When sleep is all that is left

For there the immeasurable sea
No toady of chivalry
Breathes a cold indeterminate stuff
Once dragonfoil, mooncalf, and griff.

And you my lad so brave
On the clamorous cold wave
Will sink in that blank sea lung
Unharvested, unsung.

10

> *Now for greater things to tell, give strength, O song lord, poison one, far killer with quiver of plagues, and you, old hawker of flowers, giver of unwanted gifts, praiser of the wine stem's lord, pour balmy unguent on your flowing hair, stamp your foot and cry out petulantly, for the dance draws down toward the close, the nimble feet grow slow in the poppy fields...*
>
> *And you, Ithomata, let go your loved one for a while, to come hither in her free-stepping sandals, the pure one, and shew us erotic dances, for these things we require, before your high walled kingdom is complete.*

In the morning, in the section of criminal trades, the streets awaken like an oddly punctuated sentence. Random doorways, like inscrutable exclamation points, or accent marks on words not yet written, expel charges of children or garbage. A pail slops from a window. A child is flung screaming from a door. A dog howls and is kicked. The tone is emphatic but the meaning unclear. Perhaps one could read it best in the occasional silences — listen... — but someone — a man screaming in his dreams from that dark house — a woman screaming in reply — a child joining the chorus — someone is always quick to fill them in.

On such a morning — look there — Vincent sails out from beaded doorway like pirate ship from cove. He glides past a woman carrying cucumbers, a wagon of water jars, a hag picking dung for the fire, is lost in the shadows of an alley, appears again at the sunshot bazaar, hurrying down streets strewn with sponges, silvery fish, and unnamed things, functionless and perfect, rendered up by the lower depths. The cries of the hawkers bloom in the sunny air, the myriad brown limbs tangle and resolve like a shifting veil around him, the rhythm of the cleavers in the meathouse drives him on. He is lost in silent gold-dark alleys again, then reappears by the triumphal arch on the square, where Nekko broods on old great voyages in peeling plaster while in his shadow tumblers and fire-eaters perform their smaller but no less magnificent rebuttals of universal law, overleaping and overmastering elements and gravitations; he crosses the pulsing square and climbs white steps to the broad walks of the Romans — but there he slows, nervously, and lids his eyes. For this is the sea of law, where commerce is done and reputable men rob one another in their odd formalistic way. Here he moves as the shadows move, screws his eye lenses down, disappears.

On the square sweet drinks are drunk. Behind curtains fans rise and fall. Time hangs in unbearable sunlight in the eaves. Then something breaks, some gaze turns away, and the day is dying. A breeze rises, bringing evening. The air thickens like water into which smoke surges. Column and architrave hang still in a magical suspension. There is a rustling of robes; figures emerge from a hall.

Vincent appears as from nowhere. His voice, muted and unexpected, seems almost a threat, as his hand touches passing robes.

"I have something for your master."

At once he is struck from behind, a second time, and he lies upon the ground. They stand over him in the gathering dusk, and their leader, the smooth and wily one, the governor's freedman Christopolous, his face is still. His voice is murmurous and faint, evincing that one does not rise to his post through easy laughter or passionate reply. He looks down curiously.

"And who do you think is my master, you dusty fellow?"

Vincent lies silent, veiled.

"My master receives many gifts," the freedman said. "Men shuffle their feet in the dust all day to lay his gifts beside my chair." He gazes a second longer, not to forget the proud creature who lies wounded there, then flicks his robe hem from the dust and is gone.

As every day, the melody changes with darkness. The song of heat gives way to the song of dinner. The dance of the night-beasts begins. Even where a single human sits alone in a dark room feeling for his food with silent fingers, life is renewed and death affirmed by tearing teeth. Meat is tendered up to craving meat. Both more savage and more gay than the workingmen they recently have been, dinner guests set out, lifting white robes from the warm dust of lanes, eyeing Vincent curiously, on their way to bus-stops. Doors slam. Steps pass and fade.

Soon dusk was full and the black still seeds of night were planted. Vincent rose and strode down the darkening street. It was cooler for a while, before the fast black heat of night smoked out. Through doorways the little suns lay throbbing in the grates. But darkness settled on his heart, and mad brooding.

There was a knock at my door and I ushered Wally in and told Della he was there. She smiled strangely, knowing I didn't like him, questioning me with her eyes. In the kitchen I ground up one petal of the yellow flower and slipped it into his mashed potatoes, underneath the butter.

Already some revellers drifted in warm torchlight on the square. He passed them by and sat at the water's edge, watching the treacherous familiar currents.

Wally was a bore, as always — until the moment when unexpectedly he fell to the floor beside Della's chair, as if to beg her forgiveness and plead that she return to him. He was crying strangely as in pain and grabbing for her skirt with his flippers — he caught it now — she pulled away, a look of horror in her eyes — the skirt ripping — she running shrieking from the room — a yellow liquid pouring from his mouth — the air filling with a sweet yet violent odor.
I lit a cigaret and sat back to watch as he twitched on the floor.

Flowers of rage, of hatred, of pride, surged up in the torrent. Each offered itself, but he drew back. Then the surface shifted like a lens one hadn't known was there and grew dark and troubled, like a veil tossed by autumn breezes. Phantoms he had known of old slipped by like laughter in blood, taunting him to leap out as on the sandy edge and grapple them down.

Della was shrieking in the bedroom, Wally was honking loudly, the neighbors began banging on the wall. "Alright Wally," I said, "cut it out now." I shook him. His cries grew louder. "Cut it out, dammit," I said. Finally I dragged him out the door and threw him down the stairs. The pleasure of doing it reminded me how much I detested him. He crashed against the street door, in a little while got up and left. I stood breathing the silent air of the hall, smoking and thinking. Something seemed to be darkening my mind. I seemed to be having impulses I wasn't familiar with. I couldn't tell exactly who I was.

Vague lusters pullulated into eyes and glared with a horrid dimness, like the eyes of spirits in dreams, angry, and hungry to cross over. Then something loosened underneath, the lights diffused like clouds breaking into warm rain, and on the dazzling surface each thread of the veil could be clearly seen.

I closed the door softly and began clearing dishes from the table. Now that I thought about it I could remember other times he had done things like this. So I couldn't be sure yet about the effect of the flower.

Slowly a breath pulsed behind the waters, something almost awake, almost interested, almost warm. For hours Vincent resisted the longing to leap, and tear it through at last, and look.
"He was interested," he thought. "I saw it for a moment, though he was quick to hide it."

I went to the desk and took the flower from the drawer where it lay hidden beneath the little velvet book that Quintus had sent. As I gazed at it in the late night light it seemed to throb and glow in my hand. I went into the bedroom. On the other side of a dark space Della lay like a shadowy pile of clothes or something.

"You awake?" I whispered.

"Yes," she said softly, staring with a blank look. "What was the matter with him?"

"Oh, he's an asshole," I said and sat gingerly on the edge of the bed. "You know Wally."

"Why does he act that way toward me," she cried. Then, with reproach in her voice: "What did you tell him about me?"

"Nothing," I said. "Don't be silly. You know I can't stand him. Listen — "

"Why did you invite him, then," she cried angrily. "You must have wanted him to do something like that."

I leaned closer.

"Listen, what you need is a nice cup of tea."

And brewed half a petal in her cup. Adding extra sugar in case it was bitter.

It was late when Vincent brushed aside the beads of the doorway, kindled a lamp in the pantry, and stood over her. She seemed to float in the rippling lamp-light like a corpse under water. Her dead pure radiance chilled him. The soft mounds of her breasts seemed piled up for no real purpose.

We sipped tea and talked quietly in the near dark. After an hour there was nothing left to say. She was almost asleep. Her eyes kept fluttering down and popping open with surprise when she realized I was still there. Finally I lay down beside her and dozed off.

Little storms of nervous explosions wandered over his limbs. He held the lamp down low. That used look must be gone. And the red spots in her cheeks, the whine of disease in her breath.

I don't know how long I had slept when something awoke me. Della was on her hands and knees on the bed, head lolling like a dog's, a strange glazed look in her eyes.

He fell to his knees beside her bed and covered his face with his hands, giving a little cry of — was it rage? Despair? Remorse?

Rearing up, she beat at me with both fists wildly, then was down devouring my cock and clawing at my balls. Never had she gobbled me so hungrily. I called her name and got only slobbering sounds in reply. Her head bobbed as I came.

Gradually he sank down beside her. He had not realized how tired he was, how unnaturally tired, for him, and before he knew it he had laid down on the floor and was asleep.

She lay back confusedly, come running out of her nose and clinging in white drops to her lips where, when she fell asleep in a moment, it dried and hardened.

Before dawn the lamp burned out beside them where they lay stretched out in the dimness as if dead. But soon enough the light would enter again from outside like a mist and lie over all the mountains and valleys of their bodies, entering into each tiny crevice like the crier of an indecipherable announcement, or a flock of birds whose portent cannot be read.

I sat in the dark smoking and thinking about the flower. Again, I could remember other times when Della had acted like that, so I couldn't be sure the flower had altered her behavior. In fact, it seemed to be true, as Della had kind of implied, that it was my behavior that was being altered more than anyone else's. I had previously been one to eat flowers, not to slip them into the food of others. Pondering this, I fell into a fitful sleep.

* *

Beast god, Oh god of wit,
To thee I tender up
Due portion of my writ
Some drop from the brimming cup

Oh god of beasts, we can
Take profit too from thee
And even gentlemen
Pluck from thy fruitful tree

But thou, it's understood
Who gavest without spare
Must take for livelihood
Less than is thy share

11

I dreamed that I was in a garden with high battlements whereon hung many rich pictures which I began looking at busily. But each one I looked into became a mirror and in each mirror I saw a thousand flowers. And when I saw them I felt aching desire. I awoke in the dark, veins of nervous worry twitching around my eyes.

I couldn't stop thinking about the flower.

Slipping quietly from the bed, not to awaken Della if she were still there, I padded to the desk and took stock, pulling the remains of the flower apart over a sheet of paper.

Four and a half yellow petals. An inch or so of stem. Two hard tiny green lumpy seeds.

I studied them under a glass, compared them to pictures in books, fell asleep over them.

Vincent rose early, locked himself in the room of flowers, and prepared medicines for Waz. Powders and unguents, edibles and suppositories — sweating in the heat, he prepared them with greatest care, all that were needed. Then crashing through the beads he sailed through calm seas to the palace, stopped at the end of a line, and fought with his eyes till they were veiled and still.

When I woke up at my desk the night was black against the

windows and the rooms were full of breathing. I sat for a long time smoking and thinking. Quintus had been such a bastard. What mad extremes had he gone to to get back in my book? Just thinking about it made me restless. Some compulsion seemed to grab me. I didn't even want to name for myself what I was going to do or what I seemed to be seeing of my life in some dim way as in a dream.

Putting the petals and seeds in a little envelope I slipped through the door and hurried to the bus-stop. I had no idea what time it was. The occasional cars seemed to have no drivers but to be out snuffling around on hunts of their own.

The bus hissed up and stopped like a little tame storm, gasping open, and I rode, face pressed to the window, through the guttery glitter of jangling punks, and onto the ocean of night. Someone's transistor radio played a song.

> [Baritone]   (*"Oh where do they go, my girl, my girl,*
> *Where do the rivers flow?*
> *I can only make out a swirl, a swirl,*
> *But there seem to be paths below."*)

Like a blossom proferred by the foaming current, Waz woke late in the dark hole of songs and thought she was dead. The house had lost that dominant slashing rhythm that jarred through it at will; no crashing man was tending urgent business, by which the times of day are told. Frightened, she drifted back to sleep, a brown stem tossed in the gentle but unappeasable currents.

When she woke again the leaves were swollen with rich late morning sunlight. Green sun gripped the leaves; green leaves dripped sparkling gold. From far off came a rhythm slower, older, less heeded, like the tunes the waves dance to on the sea. . . And she realized that it was coming from far off in herself. Little spines of song tingled about her.

She roamed through the shop and up the stairs, into rooms she had not quite seen in years, moving idly, like the wind, and, laying her ear lightly against one door, listened to a little scratching and a little breathing sound. She drifted to the closet, took the key from the hook he had forgotten to remove it from, and wandering back unlocked the rustling door.

And it did not swing, or glide, or turn, open, so much as it roared, or swept with invincible momentum, borne onward by an effluvium of bestial odors and piercing screams which washed over her in a stinking gush so that her eyes first opened wide, then grew fuzzy and dark as she fainted lightly on the threshold.

I pulled the bell-cord and leapt off running near the waterfront, where Quintus had last been sighted sneaking around the edges of my book. The night was warm and the air felt sweetly thick. I could tell I was near the sea-mouth, for the garbage river was cleansed by a tough salt smell. The old channel swished by as if in a clumsy hurry to reach that cold immensity and spill its burden of filth and rest in the embrace no stain can rape. I hurried toward dark water.

> [Soprano]   (*"If you don't dive in, oh lad, dear lad,*
> *You'll never be heart-whole,*
> *But perhaps the boys are sad, are sad,*
> *Who in the waters roll."*)

Quintus was tortured by dreams of opening gates; they would swing back and some dark tenant would be waiting. Shuffling through the sun-dappled dark he stood breathing loudly by the door, his eye pressed to the crack. Through gates of horn he glimpsed a cold peaceful goddess — then the baying of savage hounds approached with terrifying speed. Again, bolts were shot back and a heavy bronze door was swinging open on a dark corridor; he thought he saw grinning eyes and heard, from a dark valley, the sound of a multitude of knives being sharpened.

Doors opened but it was never her door. Yet he could hear her, drifting like a cloud of smoke from the garnered bodies of the dead, floating odorous as grease and hungry as a carrion bird, seeking entrance. A scream started at the other end of a long and distant tunnel and he ran from it, dragging his body, like a dying lover whose embrace he could not escape, toward waking. Through the red tunnel of his throat with great effort, and when it was about to leap he clicked open his eyes to a torrent of light and the scream leapt free as the hungry door which he had escaped inside was somehow still opening before him. He waited for the bark of the ghostly hounds, or the furious rushing figure and the fists.

But the light only rustled once, like a curtain being drawn, and froze to brittle silence. And he remembered: that always she wore veils, and was cold. The curtain only hung still, like stiff lace or ice over snapping jaws, and silence became like a dull song played too long. He wearied of it, and wearied above all of this void bright with fear where beasts of light ran silently north of yesterday, leaping through dimensions and times like colors through the faces of a prism. And struggling up on brittle arms, wild with old age's occasional beautiful scorn for cowardly clinging, screamed: "You, kill me, bastard; kill me, fucker, bastard!"

[Baritone] *("Oh who should be sad where sing, where sing,*
The sea-girls white and brown?
I have given my coat a fling, a fling,
And madly cast it down.")

I walked among the closed vendors' stands, the boathouses and docks, looking into the sheltered places by the river's edge where the bums slept in the summers.

"Come with me, old one," I crooned. "I will show you the kingdom of heaven." I peered in barrels, prodded old newspapers, hurried on. He would rise like a river god from the laughing waves, robed perhaps, or wreathed with sea-weed strands, and explain the mystery of the flower.

"Old river-bank sleeper," I whispered into a garbage-can, "I bring you happiness." He would lurch from the alley, an old man hungry for hamburgers, his beard shaking with raving. I would slip the petal in under the pickle and squirt it with mustard.

"Come out, Quintus, damnit," I shouted, running along the splintery dock. He would pop up like a little marionette, a watery old fruit with scared eyes, jabbering like a chipmunk.

"Come out, you old asshole," I shouted, but he would worm and squirm like a rat, eyes wild as toads, and squeal in some language I didn't understand. By god, I would cram the yellow flower into his slobbering old mouth. "You motherfucker," I shouted, "you gave me this shit — what is it?" But he only slithered away among shadows and holes with drooling sounds. I started to laugh. He only ran behind a door the wind blew shut, where I would not yet go. I lay down on the dock and started to cry.

    [Soprano]   (*"Then give it here, oh dear, my dear,*
    And toss yourself in too,
    And I for a part of a year, a year,
    Will hang it up for you.")

Now air in the high room has thickened into smoky dusk where he wanders among high meadow temples in the warm snows of his youth. On the only and broken chair Waz sits enthroned in the lambent fire of onrushing final night. . .

And it is true in part that he has remained because of the dizzying stairs, which elicited no memory except of falling; true also that when he had helped her in at last and set her upon the throne, the slow embrace of gathering dark in which she took him seemed the proper and only and joyous conclusion to whatever adventure she had set him on, long ago. But it is especially true that when he had stood in the hallway after a hundred mornings whimpering at that door, and seen the sun, and seen the stairs, and seen the street lying open beneath the window, he had wondered what had ever been out there to draw him so.

And crawling back into one of those mountain hollows which on some days in early spring, such as this one, he remembers, are locked in a magic sweetness, he pulls the filthy rags about him like cooling snows.

Now dreams sweep over him, not the deceitful memories that always have misconstrued the litany of his heart, but dreams that he has lived at various places along his way, and are not a disturbing confusion that bespeaks lost powers, but a slow song that he can sing

forever, with many familiar changes, and some new ones.
Waz sings, stirring her great smooth thighs on the throne in the gathering dark,

> Flower of love
> Do you always
> Fall to earth
> Barren?

[Baritone] (*"I'll need it not down deep, down deep,*
When the sea-girls' songs I learn,
But clasp it tight when you sleep, you sleep,
And warm it for my return.")

How many times had he swum up from these watery depths and scurried to a rat's bed by the docks, dreaming of the river king's daughters in the garbage dawn? How many poisons had he puked in this filthy stream and cleansed with the salt immensities of his tears?

And now he seemed like my life which had run away, clattering the cans, a cunning old whiskery nix disturbed in his sleep and scampering free in myriad forms I could never know — a spirit slithering through holes in the earth like wind... It seemed that I was too late somehow, that I had lost something I had never had. My life had run away and left me at the doorstep holding a ruined flower. I fell asleep on the splintery dock like a wind of dry leaves ready to burst into flame.

[Soprano] (*"Why a coat unworn gets old, gets old,*
Like a shadow on the wall,
And perhaps the sea-girls' lips are cold,
And do not sing at all.")

Framed by the darkening street Vincent's face seems lit by a kind of heat lightning behind his eyes. The other man breathes softly, his eyes frozen to bright ice in the gathering dark.

"Benefaction for thy master, noble one, even from the lowest, I bring."

"And is it thy stinking breath, pungent of alleyways, oh benefactor, or do you not show it to my master's slave?"

"It awaits him elsewhere," Vincent murmurs. Then, still more softly, "It is more beautiful than all the pharaohs' daughters." His eyes flare, passive but hungry, like the passivity of fire.

"And more diseased than all the pharaohs' dogs," the man hisses. But now Vincent smiles. He sees lust in the freedman's eyes, not lust for a woman, but lust to destroy Vincent himself. And he knows that he has him. The last words come from darkness.

"I will come tonight to inspect her for my lord. And if she surpasseth not all pharaohs' daughters, you are a dead man."

Vincent, that high notionist and rich in words, turns and paces down the blackening street.

[Baritone] (*"So if I should give that fling, that fling,*
And leap beneath the swirl?"

[Soprano] *"Then wearing your coat in the spring, the spring,*
Another will clasp your girl.")

I woke up in the grey pre-dawn light, my face swollen with insect bites, and went looking for a bus-stop.

12

(*My heart, sing again
of the lord Farshooter.*)

When first the body dies the spirit falls out with a squeak, flows gibbering to all sides briefly, then gathers itself and streaks over hill and dale — through cows even, which gives them a nice surprise — and into the grey surge, gasping.

    It's always twilight then. Slithering uncatchable things dive down deep, seeking rest. And behind them one follows on the trail of nicely surprised cows, and over the fields grows small and climbs the long hills, stooping to retrieve the brave gauntlet finally flung, the gay robes spotted with sorry blood, and arrives at the dusking hour at the grey strand where last insistent merry laughter bursts up from the breaking bubbles, or last drifting song delivers to the winds the strangled diapasons of defaulted dreams.

    [Soprano] (*"Are the boys there glad, oh lad, my lad,
                    In the tides ambrosial
                    Or is their deep life sad, oh sad,
                    Endless, lachrymal?"*)

    Bells ring in the distance and waking partway I try to count them but lose track. The church clock hangs over Littletown unbearably bright. Della rises on an elbow and tries to read it but falls back, letting the curtain drop across her window. Struggling to sit upright, a finger raised brightly, Quintus parts his lips then falls silently back. The wind tosses the treetops like waves rising over the ramparts of Littletown. The keels creak like thunder as we sleep.

("Eat this, sweetness, my lordkin, oh floramor, so ashes may blow away, so fire may be free, so electric bristle the strings. Save me, my pug, my fancy, my warrior, if you were a baby from heaven, if your daddy kissed your belly, if you spent your youth on songs. Cram this, you devil, oh expert, oh shrill hand. Your daddy trusts you, my darling, his age is as spent as yours, his brain is as burnt as yours, he drove the sword in you, he deafened you with tom-toms, he gave you for a song which you never heard and he heard neither. No more songs, no more songs, my daughter. Lie down before them, craven down, eat their filth, suffer their judgement, kiss their rod, swallow their damn proud ways, obey, surrender. Rub this. They will let go their dogs on you, they will flesh their swords in you. Drink. Oh how you destroy with submission, my bully, my rough, my veteran! Look now — they know all colors, songs that don't exist have crazed them, they snort like stung bulls. Dancing to our tune, they trample us. Your sting is in them. Their hair is on fire. They explode, fall like smashed charms from your bracelet, are picked up by silent hands where children wrangle in the dust." And closing his eyes, he takes her hand tightly—"Eat this, oh little girl, oh ruined flower" — and gives her the disease. And as he stumbles away, loosing her into the nether darkness, swallows it himself too.)

Look: night is coming.

Or is it almost morning?

Over the splashing stern — oh god! — waves drift in insoluble webs, tossing their lovely heads, then sink through the mesh of strands and are gone.

Women rise from the water at night. First their fingertips break the calm sea surface, then their hands, dripping silver. Their slender arms rise smoothly; wet hair streams across their faces. I loll my head on the bench and hardly feel the splinters tangling in my beard. They rise to their toes and dance on the waves, then fade in the foamy floor, lost in the billows, calling.

We are tangled in some giant's unkempt hair and tossed like fleas. Miles down, enormous muscles strain in the dance of life.

We waken more —. No. Sink more deeply into sleep.

Clouds pass and colors shift. Some king's daughters rise from the sea and dance. We turn the smooth mad balls of our eyes in their sockets, watching. Their breasts bob and fall as slow as the swelling silver water. They rise with a swell, then lie back in a cupped sea hand, smiling. They dart around the ship-side, calling, then pirouette daintily, as with a terrible sadness, on the wavecrests, and are gone.

Far back we see Mago with them. They comb out his hair and give him sweet lemon drinks. He laughs, throwing back his head. They swirl into white rills and foam away down canyons of laughter. We waken more, or sleep more deeply yet.

The surface of the sea grows hot and bright. Our arms ache, pulling at the oars.

The sun, that old pirate king, sears through the tops of our skulls.

Night comes.

Or is it —?

("*Perhaps the bloom is bruised, but still it is beautiful. Her eyes are almost modest. She is idiot of course? My master useth all the holes. Each will I test for him. Is this your room? Go down.*

"*Strange summer, a breeze from nowhere...*

"*Slow, slow, sweet song. What the snake has, not the dog. Bite on, tame snake, wild cow, idiot flower.... You are wet as milk and burn me. My snake is hot, he is furious, he crawls between your hissing fangs, he becomes your kind, his milky venom streaming down your throat.*

"*Wait now. Let us rest.*

"*My master will love you, little one. Feel this. His belly is not so hard. Lie back now.*

"*Your eyes go soft, go new... You are five years old, you sing silly songs. Your little hands load my weapon, at its sack of bullets working. Slow, slow, mute songstress, jewelled bird. I am your cage, your net. Ah, do your bird claws hurt me? Wait, now. . . I rise above you. My snake is hot, he is burning, he crawls into his cooling place. Ah! This hole is a dark sweet pocket in which a bright revolver fires, tearing the cloth with flame.*

"Strange night, electric breezes. . . Who is he? His room is clean.

"Can you hear me, even, idiot one? More wild and foul than the desert hyena are you; you would fuck wild dogs, could they ask you. Is pleasure a word you know? My master will love you too, for you are filthysweet — filthysweet, and you cleanse me. Inside your eyes, torn flame — don't turn away — your hair is crushed nerve fiber, from your mouth electric slime. . .

"You make a knife, make a knife of me. Turn over. Slow now, this hole my master loveth best. I flesh it deep in your sheath of dryness, a mouse defenseless in a purse of wild bees buzzing; they tear at my spine — I melt in scalding honey. . .

"Lie still, lie still, your buttocks tremble. . . In a minute I will pop it out."

We descend cataracts of unknown streams, cross billows of new ocean universes, fade into invisible eternities. . . We come to feel that our home lies behind us, in some world we fled from in mistaken fear.

Only Mago has found it, that sure pilot, that brother to waves. . .

Eyes wild as new daisies, leaping and crying among the blossoms, he throws back his head and laughs soundlessly.

Silently at the ramparts of Littletown the waves lay their gems upon the shore.

The keels creak like thunder as we sleep.

13

Whither, oh dark lords?
There is a land
Dark yes darker than life
Oh, sleep is all that is left

Night in his chains of gold
Lies weeping upon the sand
And up from the crying wave
The sun like a yellow laugh

Most insidiously does day rise out of night. Cities are fields of flowers. Silent the grey stems stand. Then suddenly the tops of the tallest ones are slashed with screaming yellow. It is as if they have changed, would fly off on high... But by a trick the yellow ages quickly to serener gold, sinks deep, and flows softly down windows and ledges. Seen from afar, the city is a field of golden flowers — not jaunty yellow, bobbing in a breeze, a wish — but stiff and violent gold, a promise grand and tragic, which it is already too late to take back...

As sun hits the top of Della's house she appears in a high window, combing her hair and singing. It is the same song she has sung before, every morning. In it purpose is cloaked as desire, and diffidence as chastity. It has melody, but the rhythm is weak, like the smooth, unruffled passage of the comb. Slowly she binds up her hair. It is quite different from her evening song, sung in veiled rooms where she shakes it down in shot tangles to the stung weeping rhythms of a heart.

For a while the air is buoyant, and the promise of the tall gold flowers seems newly made. Already, perhaps, tragic, but still lovely, still to be cherished. That is why more people sing in the morning. I have heard Della sing then, when the comb swept smoothly down. And by the river, where the stone flowers lie still on the turgid grey top, other songs. The old hamburger man where he rises among rats to a breakfast of garbage; the mad priest in the splashing stern of a boat; the song of a child drowning under the creek. Songs of departure, delusion, swaging the maculate heart, propitiating.

But morning deepens and the songs of gold grow heavy. Our lips cannot sing them. The flowerheads of our cities flame too brightly. The fever of the blooms is in us and with growing unease we begin to see that there is a price. This gold did not bloom freely; no, it is too stained, too violent. It glows more brightly than is decent. There is a payment, and somewhere a creditor waiting to collect it.

So as afternoon darkens the gold is a stain on our city. Whom did we steal it from, amid what cries obtain it? Our songs grow despondent, yearning, and, finally, base. Each of us takes the part of the creditor, demanding expiation of our sin.

By evening the affliction of our burning city has maddened us. Joyfully we give ourselves over to crime, and chant lustily the approaching night.

Faint pre-dawn light awakened Christopolous. He stepped lightly from the bed and watched her as he donned his cloak. She was feigning sleep, that was it. He thought of having at her once more, but a slight unease gripped him — what hour was it? and what was happening in the rest of this house? — and he went softly down the stairs.

By the lamp at the table Vincent sat, eyes closed, but somehow smiling. The freedman stopped silently at the foot of the stairs and watched him. Here it is, he thought, that she gets the snake. This man is cunning enough for all Africa. From some fat peasant mother she grew the cow's tits; from this man the milk of venom in them. He crossed the room and as his hand parted the beads of the doorway Vincent spoke.

"Are the dogs of pharaoh pleasing to your master?"

Hesitating unaccountably, Christopolous turned back where the lidded head still did not bother to look at him. "My master sports with dogs," he said, "until they eat one another." But the smile increased somehow invisibly, and he wished he had not spoken. "You will wait for him," he said shortly, and walked with a swift stride into the narrow street where sun would soon touch the rooftops.

Now look: over there, behind the rocks, Quintus lies like a torn brown stem beside the river. Quiet now; let's go closer. Perhaps already he has been tried in the final furnace, and will not awaken.
But look again: in the first faint light the pile of sticks trembles. So his time has not yet come.
Quintus, confused, combines two modes of morning worship, kneeling to pray, yet spreading his hands aloft.

Morning comes.
(Or is it almost autumn?)

That young scamp comes glowing in the sky, proffering yellow blossoms.
The dancers slip away from their mountain ring and creep into the woods to dally through the nonage while the seeds of dusk sprout sombre shoots inside them.

But over there, on that hillside where the first dawn light is coloring the treetops, listen, another prayer: "Oh sea that never rests and is grey and eats oh never forgiven never never forgiven sea I pray thou wilt cease washing over me into sleep and my body is gone into dreams and my brain thy voidness wished for and detested oh mother mother," and into the far country which he has lost his eyes hop wild as toads and under shadows.
Morning comes. (Or is it —?) Beasts lie down by the mother of rivers, their mouths streaked with the blood of the night prey. The first hint of light from the street drifts into the tank where Wally lies sunken in millennial sleep. Waz's eyes pop open as footsteps descend and, silent as unborn seeds, blink at the day. Morning sifts like a crooked little tune through the beads of the door where Vincent sits. Della's bed, like the false still surface of the river, billows unslept in.

Oh Littletown, Littletown, clasped to thy breathing bosom in the night we feel the waves that shake thee and in my blood. The strings go slack. The waves of night recede. I sit on the bank of the river, my sack thrown over my shoulder, and watch them.

    When will I go to them?

    (Or when will they come for me?)

Ask me how dark is life
And where does the great sea go
When night and the light of the night
Lie crying in chains of gold

Ask him if he will go
Where sun and the blind sun's light
Pouring out lies of gold
Tell me how dark is life

14

I got home just as dawn was beginning to force things back out into the open. It was like going to a job I had quit long ago. Della was gone and I didn't care. She always went back to Wally anyway, sooner or later. For once her comings and goings wearied me. I sat at the desk and would not look around. The greyness pained me. Like the flabby grey river the unmade sheets rolled and swirled on the billowing bed. The books, utensils, were scattered about like garbage on the filthy shores. The river of old men wound through my rooms and through me, rasping in and out with my breath. As I watched the light fill the room I was filled with disgust for it. My head nodded down to the desktop as rain began tapping at the window.

    Waz sat by the window and watched as the rain began. She too felt that arid pronouncement — the black wind clattering dry leaves deep in the forest of the flesh, the dogs with blank silver eyes, red foam purling their muzzles — which Vincent felt downstairs and grew lost in feeling. But here the sky's cold purity gleamed over the dying earth.

    Sometimes, she thought, the strings of her lute would glisten like that, angry and suffering like the lightning that brought tears to her eyes. And she would loosen them before they might break, and they would lie silent and dead. So, she could feel, her nerves were glis-

tening now. If their song was to be played at all, it must be soon.
She slipped through doors, dropped into darkness, crouched.

All morning I roamed through dreams. I stood at the bus-stop in pre-dawn dark and horselike things galloped by laughing. I took the bus to Wally's house and found Della there making mashed potatoes. I was on a subway and my book was gone. I ran through the cars and found one that was full of water and Wally sat in it, reading my book. I shouted at him through the glass. Putting the book down he said gravely that I was right, he had loved Della truly. He began to cry and asked me what he should do. "Give me my book," I shouted, but for some reason he couldn't pick it up in his flippers anymore, so I sang

> Well now lookahere Wally
> Dontchou cry
> Della's a-waitin'
> Where the sea-birds fly

which calmed him somewhat, and he swam around bumping sad eyes against the glass.

I woke to a torrential rain that blacked the sky. Something seemed wrong deep inside me. My life was coming apart and I didn't know why. I could barely muster a whispered prayer.

Goddess! Counsel your poet!

There was a song roaming in the kaleidoscope of dreams, a few pure notes lost in the forest of lies, and Quintus tried to hear it. But always, it seemed, doors opened on the septic scratching of his breath, that canticle of slag, as if someone leaned in to see if it was ready for the last refining.

He tried to piece it together. Had he not seen eyes like moons? No, he had not. But a crouching drop — a sparking fall — was it possible? That wing-footed god, gatherer of new-mown souls, would not enter so. Would he not step up smiling as one yawned, the afterpiece of one's final pandiculation?

And was there not some other, who enters with tentative padding feet, snuffling nose, dragging behind him a...sack? Net?! Rope?!? He could not remember.

And yet some rustling epiphany drew near, etching with terror's acid on his spine.

I sat at the kitchen table and at first the rain banged at the window, then entered unbidden and came splashing over to me. Lightning and thunder took hold in triple doses, crack-crack-cracking the sky. I was dazed, and the storm kept pulling my thoughts apart with its wet clean fingers. The lightning seemed to be entering into me, as if my boundaries were cracking open. Unaccustomed images marched through my brain. I seemed to see a field and somehow I knew that it was a field of flowers, though there were no flowers there. That was the terrible part. It had been picked bare. From roundabout the reapers surged. They sang the praises of their favorites, chanting relentlessly:

> Everywhere these flowers grow
> They are madly perfect
> Daffodils mean debts we owe
> Rose is repetitional
> Baskets fill to surfeit

The sound of the rain lay over everything like a vociferous commentary, but still Quintus heard a rustling draw near across the floor. Chills of apprehension forced his breath into shallow gasps. The rustling stopped beside his bed, and a hand touched his leg in the darkness; he became deathly still. The hand moved up to his knee with a light, light touch, then over his withered thigh. He knew it was coming for his throat, and covered his neck with his hands. But it did not. Playfully the fingers curled into his grey pubic hair. His breath bated with horror. The fingertips squeezed lightly at the root of his aged tool, which was soft and small, then moved along it to the tip. One hand came and held it while another tugged the foreskin gently back. One hand came lightly over his belly and chest while the other rubbed the pale head of his penis between finger and thumb.

Slowly Quintus's horror subsided and his eyes bulged less. So this is death, he thought, this so like human flesh. He lay still as a corpse and felt the familiar swelling within the encircling fingers. So this is how the end comes! He was glad there was no baying hound, no sack or hook — only this gentle and mysterious hand that tugged like a robin with a worm at that little flower he had thought had spilled its seeds forever...

Still unsatisfied, they dreamed of unknown flowers and these dreamed flowers drew them deeper into dreaming. Their inner fields, nourished by wild gazing, rioted with hybrid forms. From all corners of my brain a slow horde flowed to the seaside and strayed disheveled there. The flowers of their hearts now they were strewing on the waves, lacing their heads with slimy seaweed strands. I seemed to feel them walking through my veins.

Something like...an explosion of...whips — or...sails filling with wind...a kind of snapping at the masthead — rose over him, head bobbing like a snake, a vast web of flying hair, and plunged swiftly with no cry of rage and — was it? it was a mouth! — settled warm and wet around his cock, and he flailed upward, eyes popping, uttering a pitiful parrot's cry, a vague painful mumblement, a flowergentle flowersobbing Release me.

But no. That dark head — what wild goddess? — rose like a bird of death and plunged over his crying face and silenced him, sinking him deep within a mamillary sea.

> *Oh then the slow dance began*
> *Then she was pulling the strings*
> *Then the old gentleman*
> *Screeched from forgotten stings*

Quintus lay back in warm snow and one came to him with sunlight in golden hair, and they set out in the night-ships for that last and never-returned-from shore where captains wander in robes of beasts who will never be tame.

> *Oh the old have many dreams*
> *Many the net they fall in*
> *Often with many screams*
> *They fight the hands that haul in*

It was like a song, the pulse beating in darkness, the mundivagant rain rackling over, raddled with radiancy. I sat in the dark and thought of my book slipping like a wing through the rooms, roaming the highroad with a lonely cry.

> *What goddess oh god what man*
> *What girl or fish of the sea*
> *What specimen gentlemen*
> *They cry, is killing me?*

It was like the music of her lute when the strings would not tune right. The clarinet would not stop shaking dry seeds, so she closed it. Then the great harp would not stop shaking them so she smothered it with her breasts and the heaving strung vault echoed softly and softly as if departing to some far and dry distance, some meadow arid and calm.

> *Dark yes darker than life*
> *Hurry sleep is all that is left*
> *Oh call it a laugh a life*
> *A seed a throne a theft*

The string she was playing was collapsing like a cut strand of hair, foaming over like a breaking wave, and the strings of the archlute of her body were breaking dead and still.

> *When the storm had reached its full*
> *Out on some lonely road*
> *The hand that poured grew still*
> *And the still cup overflowed*

Images spilled through my mind uncontrollably. In the clearing picnickers lay with wan faces in the moonlight, a book like a little lost bird huddled wet in the bushes as the rain spattered bullet-fast.

> *One day the old just die*
> *He rattled as he went*
> *Call it a goodbye*
> *Oh call it a consent*

Finally I got up and trailed through the dark rooms, looking for my book by the flashes of sky-roaming lights. With relief I found it in a desk drawer and sat still with it on my lap as the dark got darker and the rain came closer, pouring from the crack in the vase.

Caught at last in the strands of the web she once had mastered, she who had streaked down valleys of water as we longed for her lay gasping, washed up on a foreign shore.

My head whirled slowly as if I were drunk. I was unable to tell what was going on.

> *Ask her if she will go*
> *Over the rilling white wave*
> *Where the lost souls overflow*
> *And the dead are young and brave*

15

Where was that rascally Christopolous? Governor Lucius Porcius Antoninus cursed him ten times a day and now cursed him the more, for he needed him the more. There must be a gay party indeed in the palace that night. While Christopoulos was out a-whoring, legates from the pro-consul of Bythinia had arrived, announcing that the man himself would be there, weary from fighting with the Parthians, this night or the next. Lucius Porcius, informed in his bath, lifted his great bulk at once, waved aside the simpering slaves to dry his own belly and, sailing out in white robe to ascend his chair like Jove, greeted them with unfeigned delight.

The legates swept in with an air of gallant severity, noble youths with the cropped hair of warriors and a bearing of grave fortitude from recent hardship which still did not belie desire for a holiday. As he settled himself among his cushions Lucius was excited by their look of war and leanness. Not far, not far, his colleagues toiled for honor on the field of battle. . .

His province was richer, of course. And far more civilized. But still one wearied of this limp and servile people, this fetid and stinking air, these vast and oppressive surrounding wastes in which only the broken monuments of the dreams of giants lay. Lucius had seen pits in the earth where the dead were wrapped with written words and worshipped among stuffed crocodiles, lions, and owls. Often he feared that he would die here, far from his native land, and be so abused. But his imperium had mere months to go, and Rome, the center of the world, awaited him. He shook off such thoughts and smiled, as one athletic young campaigner stepped forward and spoke with an admirable balance of confidence and humility.

"Proconsul and imperator of Bythinia to Lucius Porcius Antoninus governor of the southeastern province greetings. Having met (thanks be to Jove and Tyche) with recent success at safeguarding our eastern borders against threats of barbarians, and as the enemy has abandoned the field to us, affording us (thanks be to Jove and Mars) not leisure, indeed, and yet intermittance, we have set out with a small party for your province on the advice of tried and trustworthy physician and quartermaster, praying to find (thanks to Jove and Bacchus) in your well-known hospitality most longed-for respite from our taxing labors, in your competence and efficiency aid in procuring necessary additional forage and stipend for our troops, and above all in your companionable conversation some solace from the rough ways of the camp." And so forth.

Lucius Porcius was well pleased on the whole. The visit of a man more eminent than himself, or at least more recently eminent, was flattering; the request for monies, while always disturbing, was rife with possibilities of agreements advantageous to both, and, above all, the excuse for a round of parties in a season whose inhuman heat had buffeted into torpor even the breezy isles and odorous oases to which all but those with selfless duties to carry out had long since retreated, was a delight, a pure delight.

He set his household preparing, stinting no expense. Taking the young men into a private chamber he slapped them on their backs and said, "Oho! I suppose the wines of Egypt will be too sweet after the hardy fare of the camp eh boys?" He laughed, promised them everything, and beckoned a slave boy in a linen skirt to take them to their rooms.

Suddenly sweating profusely he lay beneath a fan which silent brown hands wielded and relished the coming evening. These lads, he thought, may well be favorites of his honor. To treat them well will do us no harm, and may someday pay tenfold...

Turning on his side, he slept through the afternoon.

It wasn't sleep but some transformative paralysis that had me. I was changing and didn't know into what. There were things moving around inside me turning lights on and off. I felt a little 'click' and my arm glowed dimly. Then 'click,' the light went on in my leg. It seemed a process separate from my will. I lapsed into vegetative stillness and in a minute they were both turned off, with an interval between as if someone had walked from room to room.

I found myself looking at a mound of clothes or something on the bed and wondering if it was Della there sleeping, as she sometimes did, arriving unannounced after a beating from Wally and leaving, almost unheard, before dawn. And yes, if I looked closely I seemed to see the mound inflating and deflating slightly, a bag of breath lying huge upon the bed. I couldn't think of what it meant that she was there. I couldn't think of what it meant that I was not.

Unexpectedly I was dozing, or somehow beholding a dream. The world rose from blankness. Days passed; years, centuries. Suns rose and fell, leaves swept by in wind, then were budding hard and green. Aeons fell into dust inside me as the lights clicked slowly off.

I sat up, frightened, staring at the vague sleeper on the bed — who could be anybody at all, really, and I wasn't sure I wanted to know — at the wind-billowing curtain, the grey room, the dark door — and at once I knew I would be slipping through it in a minute, buttoning my shirt, on my way to nowhere. My skin prickled with fear. What tyranny was darkening my mind and sending me into the streets like a nocturnal beast?

I retreated into the bathroom, groped for the light string, and turned on the taps of the bathtub.

The deep river stirred dreamily in, in its mindless and indissoluble vastness.

[Baritone] (*"Oh the sea-god runs an inn, an inn,*
On the pathways down below,
And his daughters smile, Come in, come in,
And it's never time to go.")

In the palace a riot of laughter flew free in the heat of the torches. Lucius Porcius Antoninus leaned toward the couch of the elder legate, who was on his right, then toward that of the younger, who was on his left.

"Ah, lads," he said, "when I was military proconsul of Asia (but that is a long time past), we had no villas like this to lounge in at the season's end, but summer and winter quartered in rough barracks and ate meagre fare.

"Once, when the snow was on the hills, I led a party up near Sardis, where they said the pirates were lurking with their treasure. But we found no one. . .

"I was given an *ovatio,* and Agricola praised me in the senate."

Feeling that he was going on too long, he heaved his rotundity into a merrier pose and called out, "But drink, boys, drink, dark night waits on us all," and slopped his cup dry. "My enemies were brigands who devoured the peasants. Your duty has been heavier, and needs more rewarding." He waved aside their protestations and soon the flute girls came in and the palace grew hazy with song and love-dancing. The glow of the wine lent lustre to the flare of the torches.

Soon Lucius Porcius, still yawning from last night's tippling, reeled dizzily in the haze. He looked toward the vomitorium, but held back for fear of seeming the lesser man with drink. And no sooner had Christopolous noticed this than some lowly guest began it, and Lucius Porcius made his stumbling trip and vomited greatly twice, first tickling his throat with a wild egret's feather, then reaching deep into it with a wand which, once spewed with the vinegar stream, he threw away.

Back in the hall, he cried aloud, "More food! And dancing! Bring Indian pheasants and Egyptian girls and we will feast the imperator on his way and feast him again tomorrow if he doesn't arrive tonight."

Guests cried approval, and certain ones made speeches and kept right on, standing by their couches, till the pheasants were brought and the rich hot odor of the birds cleansed the memory of wine. Then all lay back eating ravenously while the dancers performed again, stripping their veils like fields stripped bare in autumn, revealing the hills, the valleys, the forests of bronze and gold, their huge breasts wagging to the sombre thrushing of the flutes, which wailed low in the Egyptian fashion.

Haloes of colors, pulsing from the light bulb, fell like benedictions on the waves, which rose like lovers to greet the hosannas of the sun. Locked in their steamy embrace, I lost hold of time. Some primal door was opening into blankness, and I was floating toward it. But from some voc, a fankling faronade, distantly, sought me over vastures. Some sea slug or swine came sniffing, searching. Vaguely I recognized the sound of a crumpled form stirring and moaning on a bed in another room. I sat up. If I opened that door and stood dripping on the threshold, who would I see struggling beneath a net of fire? Did that bag of breath, emptying and filling, have a name? Did it have a meaning for me?

No, my mind insisted, it had no meaning. That life had no meaning. Only what I had dreamed and put in my book was real. Only the friends I had quarreled with there, thrown out and not seen again.

Only gifts brought in carriages. Flowers fallen from the sun. Only nights spent dancing in the wind on mountainpeaks.

I turned away from the door, stepped dripping across the bathroom, and picked up my book.

The dancers swept near, then away, swirling among the couches. Quaffing off his wine with a gurgling cry the younger legate reeled up and gave chase as cries of encouragment rose. Mysterious dark faces, kohl-smudged eyes, sweat-gleaming flanks and bejeweled breasts evaded him, disappearing always behind veils that whirled away, until he fell across the laps of feasters and lay back among their spilled wine laughing. At one couch a speech on love was made. Words rose, and wordless cries, mixing with the music.

Lucius Porcius watched with a worried look that soon changed to pleased expectation, then walked from the glare of the torches into the darker hall and summoned Christopolous. That man's wily face appeared from nowhere.

"Christopolous," Lucius said, "uh, Christopolous, in one way, perhaps, we might improve our entertainment, eh?" He waited for a sign of agreement, and Christopolous, blinking, raised his eyebrows slightly. "I mean, these lads, these lads," Lucius continued, "perhaps we should treat them very finely, eh?" Putting his hand on the freedman's shoulder, but gingerly, he peered at him intently and continued more softly. "That girl. . .that girl you told me of for tonight. . .is she not finer than those within?" This time he searched the freedman's face in vain. Christopolous's eyes gazed on unblinkingly, and Lucius grew impatient. "Why, what is wrong, my man? Is she not as good as you told me this morning when I paid you well for finding her? Is she diseased? Speak up!"

"There were none better among the pharaohs' daughters, my lord," murmured that impassive mask. "I am only concerned that my lord should have such lordly pleasure for himself."

Lucius japed him indulgently, giving his shoulder a little slap. "What loyalty! What concern for my well-being! Well, I will go first, my man, don't fear for that, but I see no harm in who comes after, eh?"

He paused thoughtfully a moment. "We will take these lads to her, and show them a city such as they have never seen. See that it is arranged." He turned back into the hall of feasting.

[Baritone] (*"His daughters dance and spin and spin*
Their eyelids drooping low
There is no guilt, no sin, no sin,
Only sweetest vertigo.")

I felt the rich soft cover and riffled through the precious pages. Yes, there was life in there. A face seemed to sparkle and diffuse into the light. Eyes glittered behind a shifting veil. Yet something was not happening. Dully I realized that I was not actually reading yet. In fact, I seemed to have forgotten how to read. Moving closer to the naked light I peered shrewdly. The letters seemed to move upon the page, whirling and laughing as in a thaumatrope. Dizzily I sat down on the toilet and flipped through the pages incredulous, as a fact slowly formed itself in my mind:

It was written in a language that I didn't know.

New flames leapt up as oil was poured on torches and robed figures, Antoninus and his guests, drifted through stately doorways and stood in circles of light on the broad marble porch. Groups parted and ambled off as attendants who had lain in the cool dust chatting and dozing rose and guided their masters on their way. Two or three last guests lay drunk on the couches inside. Lucius had instructed the servants to let them lie, but privately said to see that they were gone by morning, which they knew meant early afternoon. Soon all were gone except Lucius and his guests, who stood like creatures of dream in the light rippling on marble, chafing in their wait.

"Christopolous! Where is the man? Will he keep us waiting here all night?" A slave was sent off, who returned soon, bowing.

"My lords, my lord Christopolous is taken ill and has sent this soldier, who has been instructed as to your destination."

"Well, let's be off, then. Damn the man!" They strode through the darkened streets, pausing now and then to drink from a jug the soldier carried, and soon were slapping each other on the back, their annoyance gone. The moon rode high, streaming in limpid silver down the marble avenues.

"My lord Christopolous," Lucius mimicked mincingly. "Oh there is a weasel of a man indeed. I would kick him in the tail ten times a day if he were not so slithery quick. He has a lust for power, and when I am sick he lords it in my chair like the father of gods himself." They paused in the flicker of the torches to pass the jar and, glaring in their disapproval of Christopolous, drank deep and moved on.

"Why that filthy man!" Lucius Porcius continued with enthusiasm. "He knows every quarter of this city, even those it would be indecent to enter, and he comes up with the most amazing things."

But soon they passed from the Roman quarter down the long stone steps to the great square and, turning quickly into those darker narrower streets, sinister by their very profusion, where millennia of secrets lurked in the stink of the gutters, they grew silent, hushed.

Here life danced to the music of dreams, the whining strained adagio of the one bowed string that is never silent, the opium scent on the sudden gleam of the bosom invitingly bared, dusky breasts thrust out by brown hands, disappearing at once when the soldier was seen. Fathomlessly flowing like the mother of rivers, this is the district of night, glittering with a lurid diaphany, slumbering in sepulchral vaticination. . . Lucius Porcius robed his head and fell silent.

Soon, however, they had sunk to still deeper currents, streets which seemed empty only because those who lived there dared not be seen, and others dared not enter. And here, feeling safe, Lucius Porcius produced from the girdle of his robe a small flask. Motioning the soldier a few feet away he displayed it to the others.

"Here, in fact, is something which that vile man gave me. I ask you, why not try everything, eh? By this potion the pleasures of the winged boy — not to mention his powers — are so increased that they say two drops would give one success where Ixion failed, a third and the high couch of Jove who joys in thunder would be toppled by the storms that played upon it. Come, try it. Your holidays are not often, and it cost me steep, besides. Be sparing — but for your own sake of course; damn the expense. This whore will be a wolf indeed!"

They poured foaming droplets on their lips and tasted sparingly, apprehensively, that lilac scent barely cloaking the sharp cruel metal. And soon, as they drifted farther into the moonpale lost dim streets of the unknown seas, and abandoned all sense of direction, their pace increased, like their breathing, and they drank more deeply of the wine. In the face of each was a tense exalted look, and in their occasional words a distant dazedness.

[Baritone] *("Their bodice strings untie, untie,*
Their breasts are large and pale,
In the sea-girls' beds we'll lie, we'll lie,
When we've drunk the sea-god's ale.")

There were some tiny trails of shit on the edges of the bathtub. Some roaches, who probably had made them, were roaming around. Leaning my head on the enameled edge I would look them in the eye when they came near. They did not seem badly intentioned toward me. I would giggle for a while at them and then fall into a black daze and, leaning my head in the roachshit, would stare at the bulb till I lost track of time in its brightness. These periods would end when I would hear Della, or whoever it was, stirring on the bed in the other room. Then I would have a few seconds of thought before delirium set in again. In those few seconds I would address the roaches, saying things like, "I guess I've lost my book", or, "You see, the book that I found in the desk drawer wasn't mine at all — it was Quintus's. I mean — I'm not sure you can understand this — it was the book that messenger brought me — remember?— along with those other gifts." Some of them would hold still as if listening — one or two would even face me, I'm not sure if it was always the same one or two — but mostly they went about their own business. "That bastard Quintus," I would say, leaning closer to get their attention, "don't you see? I threw him out of my book, so now he's trapped me in his." Then the delirium again, and the giggles.

Finally I went into the other rooms, turned on the lights, and went through the desk, emptying everything on the floor, then the bookcases, the cushions off the sofa, food and dishes off the shelves. At some time I found myself resisting the impulse to look in the refrigerator, but it was no use. There was no place else. I opened it and looked carefully, only half recognizing them, over torn pieces of plants, vessels of fluids, piles of ground up animals. It all looked strange and horrible. Then, gritting my teeth because I knew I had to do it, I opened the little door to the freezing compartment and looked in there too. The valleys and cliffs of ice stretched out like an inviting little country, my hand rummaging there perplexed and dispossessed like some huge soft beast sure to die soon if it didn't find the warmth it was looking for. I waited patiently for my hands to warm up, then felt softly around the person on the bed, reaching in this way and that beneath the mound of covers, finding nothing. Then I picked my way over the rubble and sat in the easy chair, not thinking anything.

A pitiless and devouring light streamed over the room. Someone else and I lay like dazed fish on a trashy shore. I tried not to listen to the other person's breathing.

Lucius Porcius's breathing was too loud, locked in the hot fabric of the robe which covered his head. He stood with hands parting the beads and gazed silently into the dimly lit room where a strange man sat in a circle of misty light. What was the look on his face? Peering through the slit of his robe, Lucius Porcius could not fathom it.

A cold fire burned in the large eyes, perhaps rapture — but that was no more than he felt on his own face — no more than glowed on the faces of the legates where they stood by the table. What was the man listening to?

The soldier stepped from the back room, which he had searched, and made to strike the man with the spear-butt till he rose, but Lucius Porcius said, "Wait," and stood silent, gazing longer. There was also, not far beneath the surface, an unseemly indifference, or mockery, or secret pride. Lucius's eyes darted quickly over shelves with little boxes of indescribable small objects. There was something dangerous or foreboding about this shop, something that he could not see yet — unless it sat at the table there — but could feel in his numbed rolls of fat. He had an impulse to leave. But that was impossible. The legates must be well treated. Besides, he would seem a coward. Did he not rule this shop? Besides, the love potion burned with unendurable heat in his groin. And besides, there was the armed guard. He stepped through the beads.

"Where is the girl," he said. And Vincent looked up but still his eyes were veiled, their glittering and jittering, as he stared into the slit of cloth with a little smile.

"It was arranged," he said, "that there would be only one."

Lucius's temper flared under the goad of Eros. "So there is," he snapped, "there is one three times. Where is the whore?"

Vincent blinked slowly and somehow, with a hand that hardly moved, or with only a flicker of an eye, indicated the stairs. The soldier leapt forward but Lucius, goaded into bravado now, waved him back and, plunging into the stairway, groped upward in the dark. The girl seemed to spark and scintillate with a dingy lambency before him. And he went gladly, following that sombre luminescence into the twilight glade, as sweat raced like hot exploratory tongues about his groin.

[Soprano] (*"But what if they hang you, oh child, my child,*
Like a shadow on the wall,
And what if their lips are wild, are wild,
And do not sing at all?")

There was a darkness that I hated and a sound that I hated beneath it. Even more the torrent of light, spurting and falling in that ironic trashy baptism over all stunned flesh, enraged me. But most of all I hated Quintus. He had cringed and crouched and crawled back in my book, then made it somehow not mine anymore, but his. The lickspittle, the jackal, the reptile. The chair seemed to crawl against my skin, as if about to close a hairy grip, and I pulled myself from it.

I wandered through the rooms, remembering things with a growing nostalgia, and a breeze prowled through the window, cool from recent rain and redolent of flowers. . .white poppies and yellow verbascum on a young girl's hair and bosom — then dead leaves fleeing the winter. . . Slowly I put out the lights and felt responding clicks into darkness inside me, in the little rooms where someone I didn't know was living. Then it all was dark.

Time passed, and things settled into a new shape inside me. There was a throb of emptiness in some room where once there had been a happy glow — that was when my book lived there — and now the lights were out. But in those rifts or gashes of consciousness, those airy amplitudes where the dispossessed self ranges at dim fronteirs when the house is empty, I found that I didn't even care. I thought of Quintus and something benign and sentimental rose out of despair. In a way, I thought, we are the same now. Maybe he had cared about his book as much as I had cared about mine, and now it lay on someone else's bathroom floor. . .

For the first time it occured to me to wonder why he had sent it.

Only starlight lay on the bed, while the moon herself lurked in some cloudy corner.

"Dark bird of the desert," Lucius sang, "come fly with me. I will not rumple your feathers." He groped under the bed as far as his belly would allow, his engorged penis dragging on the floor. "Oasis flower," he crooned, "Lucius will not pluck you. He will kiss your bashful petals." Tip-toeing to the window he cried, "Dark bird of the night, fly back to your nest of love," then looked around anxiously. The room was empty. A suspicion of betrayal darted nervously through the heat of desire.

Not interested in waking whoever that was in the other room, I turned the pages of Quintus's book by the bathroom light. I supposed the language was Greek, but the handwritten letters didn't look like the ones you see in inscriptions on buildings. At the back of the book there were empty pages, and as I flipped through them something caught my eye. On one page were faint markings that were not made with ink. I looked at them torpidly for a moment, wondering why he would have skipped several blank pages to write on this one. He must have hoped that someone would not see it. I remembered having thought once that Quintus might be in trouble. I held the page up to the light and the marking, which might have been grease stains made with a finger, showed clearly. "Beware these gifts," it said, "they are not mine."

Suddenly it seemed creepy to stand naked in the sacrificial light, as I was. I padded into the other room. The bed was inflating and emptying. The breath came unevenly, excitedly, as in a tragic dream. I went to the desk, put Quintus's book back in the drawer, and sat thinking for a long time.

A great despondency took me. To begin with, my book was gone. Worse than that, I wondered if it had ever been good for me. Those wild flights, those dripping halls and beautiful sad ladies I had danced with. . . Had it ever been real at all? It had made me unsatisfied with my life, and worst of all, I did not really regret any of it. I wanted that dark face I could not see that was making me unsure who I was. The person on the bed was mewing confusedly in sleep now. I sat for a long time with my hands still on the desk top, listening.

[Baritone] (*"Oh the sea-girls' lips are still, are still,*
For they sing very soft and low
A song as frail as a shell, a shell,
That drifts through the halls below.")

Lucius tried a second door and found it locked. But the last stood open already, invitingly, and even as he passed into its moist entangling dark he sensed her presence and was hungry for her embrace. "My sweetness," he moaned, "I have found you." Holding his aching penis in one hand he felt his way along the wall. "Wild mushroom," he whispered, "where do you grow in the night?" And soon his knees bumped a bed. "Your garden, my feast," he cried, and falling on to it found her lying ready in the hot and secret dark and stroking her as the dark cave rang with moans he found her in the right position already (how thorough is that Christopolous!) and mounted her, pulling his stiff rod down and inserting it with both hands, then driving it home with wild jabs in the free and erogenous final anonymous dark. Downstairs the legates, washed in the pool of lamp-fire, listened with bated breath and would not meet each other's eyes. Vincent's eyes glitterred dimly like faroff summer thunder in his head.

The sleeper seemed to be caught in some dreadful dream, weeping and groaning, but only strangled fragments of the sounds made it back to this world. I stroked the mound of covers lightly, murmuring softly that it was alright, I loved her (him?) truly, and other things that were not strictly true, until it became still.

Then I sat at the desk again and tried to think of something to do. The wind took blank sheets of paper from the pile at my elbow and swirled them in a long stream into the darkness. It seemed to be calling me. I thought for a last time of my book, now gone out on its own somewhere unknown to me.

"Fly up, O book," I whispered, "like a white sea-bird, and strew your flowers over the cities. Leave them in the rooms where people sleep..."

Lucius was crying and whimpering and couldn't remember his name. There was an eruption and he was writhing in it, flew regurgitated from some disgusted abyss, painful and weeping, and lay still...

Soon, perhaps because of her uncanny silence through it all, he became afraid that he had hurt her. Then, remembering his anguished weeping, afraid he had frightened her. Indeed, such was the power of the potion that his erection, though less painful, had not relaxed, and already new pangs gnawed like rats at his spine demanding relief. Breathing loudly he patted her buttocks, saying, "There, there, little bird, you can still fly. Now let's try number two. Eh?" He rolled her over and reached for the wet slick hole that would come next.

I had not cropped my flower. It all came to that. I had given it to others to eat and had not tasted it myself. I took out the envelope and emptied it on the desktop. There had been the flushed-with-dreams red, the terminal cosmic not-blue — and now the pale frenzy of this almost-yellow like spinal fluid or pus. . . I looked at it closely. Yes, it glared with a pestilent eye. But everywhere on its surface, welling from underneath, a visible pulse beat and trembled. The pale seeds eddied like little beckoning whirlpools, and I knew I had to pass through them.

I dressed quickly in the darkness.

Lucius's roar of rage was unlike his whimper of pleasure. It rocked the house, and the legates sat stunned by the splintery table. Was the man such a pig as that? They knew it could not be so and, commanding the soldier to strike Vincent dead if he moved, sprang to the stairway with drawn daggers.

And when it had come clear to all of them that it was not only a man whom Porcius had buggered, but an old man, and not only an old man either, but a dead old man, and when all of them, including Porcius, had gazed with some fear and much horror on the old man's grey beard and wrinkled Greek face, and on Porcius's bobbing erection which would not go away and which was smeared not only with shit but with blood too, they descended the stairs with murder in their eyes.

And when, searching the downstairs, they found no girl, and no Vincent the Vendor either, but only bats' wings and magic flowers and odorous leaves and a soldier with his head crushed by a lamp base and dawn creeping with grey slyness through the beads of the door, they hurried out with the name Christopolous written in red anger in their hearts, into streets which one of them at least would never escape, already dying slowly into the bridebed of that lost midnight gutter where disease and death lurk in the heart of love.

[Soprano] (*"And from their lips a song, a song,*
Secret as the undertow,
Falls through our hearts nightlong, nightlong,
Cold as the falling snow.")

I gulped it down with a glass of water as grey dawn was peeking through the window and getting its knee up over the sink. Then I sat down to write a note to whoever it was in the bed.

"I love you," I wrote, then crossed it out. "Take care of the children," I wrote, then crossed it out, remembering that there were no children. Finally I retrieved Quintus's book from the bathroom floor, wrote, "Please have this translated into English by a competent translator," and put the note on top of the book on the kitchen table, weighing it down with the waterglass against the desolate scything of the wind.

Tip-toeing to the bed I kissed the sleeper ever so softly through the covers, traced with one finger what might have been the warm outline of a breast beneath the cloth, and crept out the door, pulling it shut behind me.

(*Oh barracoon...*)

Hardly had I left the house when I felt the flower pulling me. The night was rainy and that seemed right. I bought a ticket for as far as my money would go and, happy and excited about my new life, dozed off as the bus roared out of the sleeping city into the dark countryside.

16

(But O my book, stay never long in one place but always be rising away, away, from the reaching hands. If they wake up and call, "Who's hiding in the corner there?! Alright you!" just flap your wings and, giving a sweet cry, be gone through the window.)

(Dear god, take Quintus in,
A man whose only sin
Was silly thoughts. Or take
His soul at least and make
A little bed and fit
Around and over it
Clean sheets, that he may rest
Till at full table blest
With heroes' company
In pious revelry
He may shyly sit
And smile on whom he writ
In fourteen books right dull
My god! but courageful
And well-intentioned. Kiss
His little nose, remiss
Of what he shuddered at.
He sure deserves all that. . .)

II

1

Morning. Della sits in her high window. Behind her the bed is neatly made. It has not been slept in. A look of sorrow darkens her face, of pain and sorrow. When the sun rises, she reaches for the comb.

Now the early sunlight comes, paler than gold, almost true yellow, winding through leaves over rooftops. Falling through the window like a tamed bird, it lightens her hair. The translucent brown shell of the comb shines yellow also, in the hand which rises from the lap. Down the hand pulls it. Tugging at the strands, it cries; grating at the strands, it cries for its deep sea home.

What is that call of inquietude, that cry of unspendable gold fretting over housetops in the waking town? Soon, if her hysteria passes, or if it mounts high enough, driven on by the plaint of the captive nagging comb, she will sing, to drown the comb's cry.

But look there, away from the town. . . It is morning, and by waves' edge Vincent sits, in early sunlight, on a rock. Ocean breezes range his robe-folds on the sand. He gazes far out at the tinctorial raw unfaded blue of the sea. *Procax! procax!* the waves cry in their idleness. *Procax!* in their idle churlishness. Around him clatter white foam and lanky ling the waves cast up.

And over the distant horizon, look, the sun, gasping a glaucous cue for the sacred sea. On the waves the cold dancers are ready, on the saline brackish blue of the waves. There flutters from their robes a spinous rill. Impetuous in their wry senility they laugh and chatter and will start too soon.

The comb tunes on the unresined gold strands. Della hums, in an alto voice unnatural to her, testing the pitch.

And — hush now — from far off — listen! the beautiful jagged pausing irregular rhythm of terrified feet. Someone runs in the dark canyons whose tops will soon be shot with brightest gold. The mad howls of machines — it is time! Morning, and there is much that we must do! Hush now — the steps draw near the door. . . .

> Get up there! Don't you see
>   He's calling you and me
> The time for secret darknesses is gone.
> The sun is at your bed
>   Knocks at your silly head
> The sun, that glorious man, that pimp, the sun!

Oh, what is that spinosity of rills, that glory of arrowshafts over rooftops? Leaning on an elbow, we rub our eyes. It is not right that the sun should come bouncing with giddy beams. It is not right that he should come rolling in a torrent of fire down streets we have made pure at last in the criminal dark! Through patient work, we became truthful. Then he came bouncing.

If we slept on, if we just refused, then morning would be beautiful too. . . Stunned gold dripping from the rooftops. Rivers of yellow blossoms in the streets. The billowing and the heat of the blossoms as they piled up to our windows, covering our beds in gold suffusion where we lay, never needing to rise, so fine a rest is this. . .

> (*But we must all agree, you see,*
> *Della and Wally and you and me. . .*)

Morning, and Della twitches in weeping gold. Stunned birds lie limp in gold pools on windowsills. Della is washed in the river of molten dreams.

    Get up, you slugabed!
    We all wish we were dead
    But morning hurls cold fire on the house.
    Some fool admits it's day?
        Now there's hell to pay
    You might as well get up before it's worse.

    Morning! Oh Della, sing to me, you bitch. Roll over and let me taste your weeping mouth. They are drowning us in their yellow river, my dear, dragging us over the splashing gold shores, and you, you never were right anyway.

    Morning is like a weeping song that Della sings when her lover goes, buckling his belt as he zips through the window at the cuckoo's cry. Her eyes drip a most grievous gold, fit for an ancient whorehouse...

    Get up, for heaven's sake!
        You don't look half awake.
    The sun will take some sleepy girl to wive.
    That burning yellow ape
        Has got a bent for rape
    So cover yourself up, and look alive.

    Lolling his lobate head, Vincent lills from sun window. Her liplets lapping at the ling. "Loach," she cries. "Lobcock, lither!" Seeking liss, he lippens to his liripoop. "Lob," she cries. About her neck, like wattles of a fowl, the lionced kirtle. "Lameter," screams. The lampas like fowl wattles round her neck. He lasks, descends, goes out to lilly-pilly, lants.

    But she, she, luctual by the lum, cries, "Looby," cries, "Lusk!" A velvet loo she dons, a lepid loo, and lollops in fowl wattles by the lum. He lumpers up the loke.

    Wind lins. The lade grows lissome. Lagly looms she in the doorway, liplets lilling on the ling.

>   Get up, you silly thing,
>   No time for arguing,
>   The pimp is standing right outside your door.
>   He shakes his bag of gold,
>   This morning you've been sold,
>   Get up, he says, get up, you little whore.

I wake up on the bus as morning is splashing in yellow tears across the sill and, raising the window, lean out and sing,

>   Get up there, don't you see
>   The sun got up and we
>   Mustn't let him see us still abed,

but dazed by drugs and boredom soon grow sleepy myself and before the light has filled the roaring bus doze off.

>   *He got up and he ran*
>   *Like an angry man*
>   *Across the sky above your sleepy head.*

2

When I wake, the morning is floating away in sad gold through the forest and, gazing at it, I seem to see Della there. She is dancing, tiny and faraway, in the drifting light. The winds toss her hair, and her skirt floats over her knees. . .

Della, dead girl, fallen dancer, you are a dark moth gliding over me, truly you are. I try to sleep and you blink foolishly, waiting to be seen, great unwieldy creature not made for death, only too clumsy to avoid it. . .

It is afternoon and quietly I turn the pages of my book.

The readers of any book must take it into account that the author felt a certain actual hostility toward them. I mean, he lied because he detested them, because — yes yes. . . A new audience is in order.

I chuckle and lean my head on my hand. Della, Della, you are dead, and that is in order. In the place where the knives are kept your handprint shows you found an answer. But time still passes, Della, very fast. Leaves whisper the sadness of their changes in declining sun.

I get up and wash my hands at the sink, then go to the window.

We are just going to forget about the first part of this book. It was all lies. Now I am going to start over again and do it right.

The leaves are dancing in their way that I haven't deciphered yet, whispering slyly of seasonal change, and answering, I do a little dance in my room. They turn, bob, turn, along with me.

> (Get up, oh little world,
>   We've womaned and we've girled
> And now here's morning creeping up the stair
> He winks his eye of gold
>   He laughs all wild and old
> His hungry hand comes knocking at the door.)

Daylight is failing and the colors of my room are softer and sweeter now. Only the last rays still glide across the ceiling, saying goodbye.

Goodbye, goodbye.

And, yes, I knew it, the dark is spilling like a powder from the leaves now, a bodiless rustling descending in immaterial slumber. Night comes, magnificently repossessing his dominion. The darkness flows in like cool waters, so smoothly, so silently. . .

Sunk in the cold north salt, Della may float now, surely. Look, some pieces of dirt have come off from her arms and hang suspended in the water. If no other bodies changed, they could float there forever, like ice.

Della's hair was full and fair, fell down her shoulders once like a rush of words. . .

Hush. . . They are burying her now. . . The cold ship glides over the crystal sea. We stand straight and sad. *Della!* Is that you on the shining sea? Scattered among the scattering layers, she may float forever now. . .

My head is getting powdery. There is music of darkness, and silence, last silence of day. Papers rustling. A drip.

She rises from the bed, turns toward me. "Here the marascas grow," she whispers, and I take her breasts in my hands and kiss her hot wet mouth.

So suppose you took a journey, Della, a long way off, and now ice holds you in a glacier in the North. Slowly you sink down deep in the great ice-bed. How long till all warmth is gone? Could we reach you first, digging in with our axes of dreams to give you what you need to live in utter cold? Or have you forgotten us so completely that you cannot even be seen, and we will stand in your very pocket, perhaps, crying, "Della, Della," and only the waves will answer?

Night descends, and a gnawing begins in the wall. Circling the room with hushed breath I find it at the entrance and lay my ear against the door. It stops and listens, little paws raised trembling, ears erect, whiskers twitching. . .

I wash my hands and lie on the cot. Characters from my book appear like dust floating in sunlight, gasping to rise up. As I enter the dream with them my breath grows slow and loud in the darkness.

3

On the other side it is day, and hot sun streams through the dusty air. Outside the window squirrels leap through the elm branches, twisting among the sun-shot leaves. Behind the glass the woods glow gold and still.

It is autumn, the bear's time. Between the elms the air heats bronze to gold. On the path summer lies like a golden cup. We are sad, for we know it has long since been drunk dry. That was summer's deception, the promise of glaring yellow. Now we curl up in closed rooms and stare.

But our sorrow at spent gold is happy, too, for the winter's sleep we walk toward seems a law. At our windows the boughs hang heavy with bronze suffusion, promising peaceful beds where the bear may rest. Heavy and slow, we lumber down the path. And sleep seems a wise and bearable law fashioned by someone who knew that nothing else could end the gold of autumn.

But look: the wind grows cold; gold slips away; between the elms air freezes gold to white. A broken face of white finality drifts without a glance outside our window. I stir, deep in sleep. The cave grows dark and in the dark I hear the breath of beasts. It was a trick! Moaning, I dart and stare. Autumn also deceived! Even the bitter inner heat of outrage will not warm us now. Even the brain is growing cold and still. Even the heart sinks down with no desire before the void swirling white which we know now is no law, for it has no reward for obeying.

I awaken in the dark and my heart is beating fast. How do they live, those people in my book? How brief their little lives! How the pages of whiteness close down around them! The veil is at their mouths and they scratch at it and gasp for breath. Slowly they grow quiet.

At last they are asleep.

I go to the sink, then to the door and make sure it is firmly shut. Then to the desk, and sit.

Finally the others are asleep and the one whom dimly you perceive to be yourself stands stiffly in a room, sits stiffly on a chair, breathing with open mouth, like an animal. The mind neither clouds nor comes clear. Shadows shift on the arena of some struggle. You cannot think of what they mean, these lives around you. You cannot think of what it means to be awake. Helpless we sit in rooms that we have made and are surprised when the cave grows cruel and still, when the hardest of all sounds is heard from its deepest darkness, the slow snarl of the brute that drives the body even when it has laid down gasping for final rest.

I go to the dark window and see only my reflection. But wait. Look again.

What murder is in that look? Who glares from behind my face? A flicker of darkness pulses across my chest.

I am the veil. Someday I must tear myself through.

We have not long in the arena of violence. We have not long on the forest path. Our brains will not live. What we love will not live. What we remember dies. The wind on the forest path will not remember us.

We are creatures of a day, and that day the white flesh binds with strident cellular commands, the excremental guts strangle round with their burden of suffocating filth. We squat like dull beasts and scratch at what lies between our feet, for that one day before we must fall down and be forgotten.

Toward evening then we note with some surprise that the air has ceased glowing with gold, the forest, the forest no longer throbs, no longer is drenched with brightest gold. And toward night, as the dark settles in, we will eat and think to sleep and rise again. And when the night is full and the last bells ringing will lay the soft and deceitful flesh upon the mattress which it has demanded and where it will kill you, lay it down to no pleasure but groggy sleep, and lazily, idly drift off where the white flakes fly and all color is gone and the dumb beast shakes loose at last the dull burden which it hates and comes apart in the final relaxation which, we realize too late, is all it ever wanted.

    The window is dark but my eyes see gold of morning somewhere, off to the side where they can't directly look. There seems to be a knock, and I stagger up. The knock comes again, insistent, and I open, and morning appears like an old acquaintance I had hoped I would not see again, standing uninvited in the doorway, his greasy fire in his hands.

    And I wish I did not have to let him in.

        Now Della now's your chance
           To do your weeping dance
      We're looking and the day is coming now
      It's lighting up your bed
           Get up or you'll be dead —
      An eye appears beneath her arching brow.

4

I got off the bus at a little snowy town and checked into a rundown hotel. While climbing the stairs to my room I glimpsed, for an instant, a girl's face floating in the yellowed light of a kerosene lamp. I recognized her with amazement. It was the face of the dark little girl I had fallen in love with as a child in school. Her door closed softly behind her. Later I asked the desk clerk who she was and as he answered I noticed that he was older than he looked, or maybe younger than he looked, and something was wrong, or maybe something was right, about his eyes.

She was his daughter, he said. And she mopped the floors. And he fixed me with a gaze of burning brightness that I could feel on my back as I walked out and down the street, stopping people along the way and saying, "Do you know an old man like this?" — then make a goofy face.

There was a river that was almost frozen and as the last light lingered like crystal about to shatter a little boat poled in with baskets of fruit. Their color was brighter than blood, yet like it — like the blood in dreams. They smelled putridly sweet.

"Marascas," the man said, as if I had asked.

I bought a little basket of them and walked home in the early darkness tasting the dark bloody flesh. White flakes danced in the yellow flare of old streetlamps. People were leaving shops or offices after late work or dinner, bundled up in a friendly comfortable way, calling goodbye to each other, homeward bound. Soon I was alone on the streets. I stopped under a golden streetlight and composed a little note on a paper that the snowflakes wrinkled.

Back in the hotel, in the wavering light of the corridor, I positioned the basket and note outside her door, knocked softly, and hurried back to my room. The note said:

> If you sleep too deep I will waken thee
> Is the load too heavy I'll take for thee
> If the pain too sharp I will ache for thee
> O to hold the mop with thee

I sat on the bed and smoked nervously. From next door a kind of crying or crazy whimpered singing came in an old man's voice. Every now and then a rasping breath approached the door between our rooms. Someone would stand silent, then shake the knob lightly as if to see if it was locked. I wondered if it was Quintus. Anyway, whoever it was sounded deranged. I propped the chair under the door knob and fell into a nervous sleep upon the bed.

I was on the river floating in the slime, fighting something wrapped around my face, when a sound in my room brought me upright. There was an instant of wavering light in which a girl's head turned with streaming hair and disappeared before I could see her face. A door closed softly down the hall. I was in total darkness.

I felt my way down the dark hall to her door and there was a slight breeze as it swung open unurged. In an instant her touch was at my arm, gentle and familiar, drawing me in. Hardly was I through the door when I smelled the sweet odor of the bloodfruit and passed willingly, even eagerly, into the dark, knowing that this was what I had wanted above all things. A hand lit a candle and I saw her in the bed, glowing like the fruit in the basket beside her, moving and sitting up as if to come toward me, the sheet falling away from her naked breasts. Her mouth was opening and blood was pouring from it. But no; she held a marasca in her hand and had bitten into it, that was all. Suddenly spewing bloody seeds she screamed at me in a language I didn't know, her face contorted by pain or rage. Arms grabbed me from behind. I struggled free and ran down the corridor, ricocheting off the walls in the dark, and into the room I thought was mine.

Breathing hard, I put match to candle. By its flickering light I saw a little envelope thrust halfway under the door to the next room. Picking it up apprehensively, I studied it by candleglow and saw a name not mine, then in an instant realized that it was not a name not mine but simply a script that I couldn't read — in fact, it was the familiar whirling script of Quintus's book. I banged at the door, then tried the knob, which turned easily, went in and found an empty room, torn papers scattered about and the window open.

Hurrying into the night I went through the snowy streets and asked the late wanderers, the thieves and drunks, and those on searches of their own, making the goofy face. And yes, some had seen him, but it was always just the floating hem of his gown as he rounded a corner, the gleam of his old eyes as he disappeared into an alley, his wild laugh rattling among the trash cans, and he was gone.

First morning light had come when I pushed open the hotel door and went to the desk. "The halls were dark," I blurted out as if meaning to say so much more. And, yes, he said, and I could not penetrate the veils of his eyes, yes, the hotel had been dark because his daughter was sick and had not refueled the lamps. She had eaten some rotted fruit, he said, that brought on delirium.

I drifted in a daze to my room, remembering the taste of the bloodfruit with dismay. In a delirium I must have hallucinated things — visits, letters, invitations — and foolishly intruded into his daughter's room when she was with her lover, or maybe her husband, who tried to protect her from me. And I had seen her naked. Suddenly it all disgusted me. I expected the police at my door any second. Gathering my little bundle of things I paid at the desk with downcast eyes and barely had time to buy a bottle of wine when the bus roared in as if from nowhere; I jumped on as the wheels spun gravel, found a seat by the window, and fell at once into a troubled sleep.

Later I made my way to the restroom and fumbled in my pocket for the bottle. A little envelope fell to the swaying floor. On the outside was the name not mine. Inside was a little slip of paper written in the writing I couldn't read.

I went out at once and saw green fields through the window. The passengers told me I had slept for almost a day. The driver had changed. No one could say what little town I had gotten on at. As I sat in a daze and thought about it, it seemed that the hands in the dark were not actually grabbing me so much as reaching for my wallet. I cursed the lot of them as the bus roared on, and above all Quintus, whose reappearances in my book were becoming increasingly unpleasant.

But later, as night fell and the air conditioning produced its clammy chill, I could think only of the hot weight of her hanging breasts, her glowing arms and shoulders rising from the snowy sheets, the cleansing flow of putrid sweetness from her mouth, like a menstruation. At last, finding the dark of strangers unbearable, I went back to the careening rest room, sat down, and sobbed for what I had nearly found, or had nearly lost, drank the rest of the wine, and toasted her and me in drunken songs while the dark bus roared on to its unknown destination.

And many the field and many the town
I roamed in when the earth was green
And many the bed where I lay down
And saw what I should not have seen
Her flaming hair her flashing eyes
The circles of her breasts and then
The cracked vase where her secret lies
Where I must lie down once again

5

Alone in the high room I sit thinking of you. A squirrel comes up to the window. You were like all small things. Puppies with their faces pushing into mine, birds with their hearts so fast. Little beautiful things that look in the window in passing and are gone with their swift so beautiful bodies flying flying. . .

You were like all lovely things.

It is difficult to explain what has happened to me since I began this book. How many have I looked for on the river? When I found them, what was it? A flutter at the heart, a mouth pulsing at the hand. A tenderness that stuns the brain, casts a mist round the head, and we fall.

Look now. Listen. I'll grab you and show you. Step out of this page and loop hands in your hair, hold you close, kiss your mouth eyes mouth. I'll tell you something true and you'll be happy. You'll know something's true. . .

My head nods down into stillness. Lips pulse at the hand. A darkness comes up all around.

I want this world to be over.

> You, listen, gracious spring,
> Consider again
> Your flowers boughs meadows
> For my heart is dying

Suddenly awake, I notice a loud breathing in my room. I quiet my breath, but the other is still there.

Ah!

It is the fan.

I reach carefully for the lamp switch. Whiteness comes, and with it a little yellow.

What makes my heart beat so?

I stir around the room.

That gnawing or clawing begins somewhere and I circle the walls with hushed breath and locate it in the corner near the door.

So someone is trying to get in.

I wonder if it is you, my beloved.

I splash myself at the sink, and sit at the desk, in the cooling breezes. Soon I am leafing through pages and the night gets late. The moon sets. The stars glitter coldly out.

I work at my book.

6

[Wally] "Oh the morning is golden and true, dear,
 And the sunbeams are winsome and bright
 But don't let them get hold of you, dear,
 They will kill you, they'll kill you, that's right.

 "Oh the night is the time meant for you, dear,
 When the angels of darkness float down.
 See their eyes, how golden and true, dear,
 Feel their hands, how they're pulling you down."

[Della] "Oh the morning is golden and free, dear,
 And the sunbeams are crazy and bright,
 But I won't let them get hold of me, dear,
 No, I wait, I must wait, for the night.

 "Then the darkness grows thick as the sea, dear,
 And the angels grow wild as the waves.
 They are waiting for you and for me, dear,
 Calling, 'Come, to your loves, to your graves.' "

I remember meeting Della when she had read the M section of the dictionary. It was springtime and the bus was passing through golden grain fields under a blue sky. Quintus was in the narrow aisle, dancing his watery old man's dance. I woke up as the bus was entering a crowded station, rushed by him, and got off. It was a hot day, and the streets were full.

I walked past Easy's Place, where crippled songs fell through the oily air, the Empire Theater, which was closed and boarded up, and to the el. When I got there the powder of evening was sifting through the air. I watched the entrance to Della's building while warm breezes came up from the ocean. A train passed overhead, rushing like a very angry angel over the rooftops.

I walked quietly through the shabby hall, climbed the stairs, and listened at her door. I knocked softly. Then I went in.

She was on the bed, gleaming white and alchemical in the dusk, and very stoned. I lit a cigaret and closed my eyes where little suns were still struggling and dying. In the greyness she passes to silver, then, shaking down her yellow hair in the dark, to gold.

"The motmots are crying," she whispered, smiling the way I remembered. .

"What?"

"Mormo," she said.

"Are you alright?"

She closed her eyes in slow time, smiling. A little wind puffed through the window, stirring the plastic curtain.

"Where's the works?"

"In the bathroom," she said, then whispered, "where the miltewaste grows."

I went into the bathroom where the miltewaste grew. Then I came back and sat on the musnud by the bed.

"Mole —"

"I saw them," I said.

"Mole —"

"I know," I said. But she had to say it.

"Molebuts are swimming in the bathtub."

She moved nearer and I put my hand on her chest, between the breasts. "It's like that spring," she murmured in the silence, and I could hardly hear her. "We would walk through mother's house —do you remember? The mutes would be howling."

I lay down beside her and listened to the howling of the mutes. We both lay still for a long time and the edges of things started getting blurred. The maleos stalked out and stood stiffly here and there in the field of grey madnep and masterwort. They arched their heads to one side, eyeing the blossoms. Then they began to eat, clicking their beaks, and I closed my eyes. Slowly at first, then with an inexorable onrush like doom or fate, the bed began to shake and roar. She hid her face in my shoulder. It shook forever with an awful roar. Then at last the room was dark and still. In the deep mouth of silence came only the sound of beaks clicking off the blossoms.

She said something.

"What?"

"Meacock," she murmured lazily, lost in the dream of words. Then, "Mome."

"I'll mousle you," I said, and tugged her gently.

"Muckna," she murmured. I unbuttoned her blouse of merv slowly. The marikinas shrieked from the corners and swung from lamp to chair to ceiling.

"Oh, maunzer," she said, and laughed a very rich and abandoned laugh, and a sudden flitting burst where the martlets, night flyers, flew.

Sitting up, she unmabbled herself, and the gold began.

"Makebate," I said, and she swirled her lovely head till all the gold shot out and poured it like sun-swollen rain on my chest and shoulders.

"Push off," I commanded. She shook down her hair in shot gold.

The mohoohoos began bellowing in the bathroom.

"Push off," I said, "the massoola."

"Don't moither," she said. She was down with me now, kissing my chest, unbuttoning me. "Meng."

We pushed off in the massoola for the land where the marascas grow. "Store provisions," I said. I was admiral. "I'll row." And our little boat rocked into the astral vastures, under the stormy vaultages of heaven.

The mohoohoos rushed in one minute late, bellowing goodbye, their marshmallow bodies bumping softly in the crowded room

*(Here the marascas grow
Under the jetty
We'll have a bungalow
Where the marascas grow*

*And wind can blow and blow
It's still so pretty
Where the marascas grow
Under the jetty)*

7

Oh, slow, still dancer. Watch her as she rises.

I sit alone in the high room and dreams of women torment me.

The sink is dripping and I arrange a newspaper under it and sit on the floor for a long time reading it as the water seeps through.

Then I sleep, and it is morning.

Days pass in distant sweetness, like a dream. The sun sweeps daily across my room and back and I lie beneath the fan and smoke for hours, delighted by the barren worlds that form in floating miniatures of mist and, mezzotinted by his festive gold, rush off on the breezes. The ashes of universes grow thick upon my floor. Eternities issue from my lips and I am silent.

I write letters, then sleep through the hot afternoons.

Usually I awaken as night reaches its cool grey fingers through the window, clasping all things in its free, its inescapable and grand free possession that always I wish will not end. Half awake upon the cot, I lie still in the luxury of that coming which disposes all things to itself, then get up in the final half dark and sit, my hair ruffled by the fan, and write more letters, most of which will be thrown away. I pace sometimes, smoking, and think about the colors of this room. In the gentle yellow light from my lamp they grow still and pleasing, and the dark night presses all around. My room hangs like a breath in the air. Then my eyes might fill with tears from no apparent cause, or abruptly my thoughts disperse and my breathing become audible. It passes, like a moment of dizziness, and I sit at my desk and try to remember what it was that linked somewhere in the dark to a memory and a response.

I lean panting in the heat. Waz stoops by oasis pool. Like jewels are her eyes. Lowering the veil, she turns away her face. Jewelled birds fly out in her breath and freeze in fan-like shapes upon the air. They lie as if painted upon the green leaves. On the blue of the sky between the leaves they glitter. But now across their wings dark streaks appear. The picture begins to darken.
Someone is filling it in.
Finally it all is dark.

I pull the bell-cord, get off by a little muddy river, and swim down. At the bottom, in a golden room amid the wilderness of turds, Quintus sits. He is eating dinner, but his senile head keeps falling in his plate.

Seeing me he gestures wildly with his fork. "Oh ye war-impetuous son," he cries. His head pitches forward and rises with food on it. "There was one whom the king slew, born to him of fair Creusa where the lovely streams of Lindus meet the sea, beside the marches of the battle-biding Thasians and the Lycian heights renowned. . . the maidens with delicate thighs. . . their lovely hands. . . beguiled daughters of the river king. . . his flaming hair. . ." His old head bobs helplessly, accumulating layers. I swim closer, curious, but he turns quickly with a food-covered laugh and dances with strange high steps through the golden door.

I wake in my seat and gaze through the window. Darkness. Rain splashes the glass and the highway. A brooding melancholy takes me, like too sweet wine. The bus churns on. Treetops brush at the windows. It is night, morning, night.

I get up in the dark, feel my way to the door, test it lightly, then to sink and splash water, then to desk.

I am going to confess something now.

It is that I imagine things in this room. I mean the floor shakes the bed becomes a seat the trees are rushing by it is moving not away but toward and I know where. Stop. Or the boards breathe loudly and I cannot stop them. Stop. I pretend I cannot stop them. Then the breath becomes an engine the floor is throbbing the night is water the tide is full. Stop. You probably don't understand this. That gnawing commences very faintly furtively and I still my breath and listen as it moves through the wall. I scurry no not scurry that was imagined again I should stop these letters now but I am beginning to need them move walk on two legs like you no not you like anyone and find it slowing zeroing hovering just on the level of my heart above the desk. And *pound*. This is disgusting. I was going to say (I will start again) I was going to write (forget that at the beginning) I was going to rise and raise, almost, my arms in as it were not greeting no not that I was going to raise my arms beside the window that would be a dance indeed.

I flip a switch and my room springs up, rectangular and bright, like the interior of a bus, the last night bus through the trees, but I strive against it.

I take up the pen.

> *Dorotheus the Theban*
> *who killed his body*
> *before it*
> *could kill him*

Yes it is like strong music. I write it slowly and painfully, drops of perspiration showering the scratching pen.

I am trying to reach you, my dearest, from behind this little pen, these painful scratches. . .

At last, breathing rapidly, I lay my head on the paper and suffer the bombardment of light. Quickly it flattens out like a river and flows like sleep into a surface where reflections are cast. I see Quintus dancing on the wave-tops faraway. The night winds blow over him and the moon comes out and glints from his hair and beard. He steps high on the parade of images in the water.

Della turns toward me and smiles. "So you're no fool," she says as if conferring an imperishable title. "No fool," I say. "Here's wine." And pausing we both drink deep of the dreamy darkness. She leans over me, tendering now a priceless and intransmutable treasure, and kisses me with a mouthful of wine, her squirming tongue asserting its wordless message from the roots of life. I see her on the cot, glowing arms rising feverish from snowy sheets, the hot weight of her hanging breasts, the cleansing flow of putrid sweetness from her mouth. . .

She stoops by oasis pool. Jewelled birds fly out in her breath. . .

Across the picture dark streaks appear. Already she is like one whom I do not know, a face that I scarcely saw before the dark threads pulled it down, away.

I turn away before it can all be dark and go to the window. I watch as night spreads over the forest, slowly cleansing the riot of images from my mind.

And soon I will do my little dance, to show how the stars move and that we are not so very serious after all. . . And yes, I am floating down now, goodbye, goodbye, a little leaf on the wind, lost among fading stars, and there is darkness, and coolness, all around me.

>(Oh the deep undertow
>Of the shore where marascas grow
>The rocketing vertigo
>Of sea round the jetty
>Where the marascas grow
>It's oh so pretty)

8

So you're no fool, she says
No fool, I say, here's wine
And soon we are ablaze
With fires from the vine

The songs were brave to fly in the tameless fever of the lights. "How can you live in that filth," I said. We sat by the bandstand where the music played. "The damn trains and the damn cigaret butts in the bed." Beneath the flying music was a wash of voices. "How do you put them out on the sheets anyway. That's what I'd like to know." She sat close, leaning on me, her hand in my pocket.

Her yellow hair lay like an accusation on my shoulder and chest.

"I need you," she said dreamily, "to come in overalls every day and sweep the floor and take the garbage out. And we'll all live together in a little yellow house."

"And it'll be clean," I said. I didn't ask who all was.

"Maybe."

"Too fucking clean," I said. "And those damn birds won't click around the field anymore. We'll flush them down the toilet."

The music droned on in its entranced fanatical vision. We sat still and let it scrub us hard for a moment. Then we left.

On the sidewalk everyone was walking raptly and quickly as the night grew late.

"The people are rash," I said, "to walk on the innaccessible light." I patted her ass.

"They look like they're dreaming," she said.

"So those going toward dream one thing," I said, "and those going away another."

We chose those going away, for it was not very late yet, and merged with them, finding a slow spot in the traffic where she could lean on me.

"What usually happens," I said walking, "when they put them out on the sheets, is that they burn themselves up."

"Some people can't be burned," she said.

"Anymore?"

"Just can't," she said, and then repeated it: "Can't."

"So what happens to them?"

"The landlord just finds a spot of grease."

"Does your landlord know to look for that?"

"He doesn't know shit. He is an ugly little man with a fat bottom."

"Like yours," I said, and patted it again.

"It'll eat your hand," she said.

"It can't eat," I said.

Nearing a liquor store we peeled off, bought whiskey, and were walking again with a bottle in my pocket. She leaned harder, trying to slow me down.

"The whiskey man didn't like you," she said.

"No," I said, "it was you he didn't like. He hated me."

"Of course he liked me," she said. "All men like me." And she wasn't leaning anymore.

"As admiral I say they do not like you," I said. "They may want to fuck you, but they despise you. Except me, of course. I would never fuck you. As admiral I dissolve your marriage to that whiskey man."

"We weren't even married," she said as we passed in front of a hot dog stand.

"They're selling the hot dogs fast," she observed.

"Yes," I agreed. "They're inspired in their work. The people love the hot dogs because if they eat them they can fly."

"They don't love the hot dogs," she said. "The hot dogs are obscene."

"Very late, when the place is closed," I said, "the hot dogs fly."

We turned the corner and walked down the avenue beneath cool trees, drinking some of the whiskey. We crossed the highway and a stiff breeze rose from the dark.

"The beach is brave," I said, "to lie still in the slaughter of the waves." Some birds slept on the water, then screeched away when a wave would try to get them, then slept again. She stumbled and sat down.

"You think you're brave," she said, "that's what you mean. Isn't it."

I lay down on the cold sand and she sat beside me. She tilted up the bottle in the dark and I watched as she drank for a long time. Then I drank for a long time, while her voice came as if being carried on the wind from faraway.

"When you say someone's brave you mean you're brave. When you say someone's beautiful you mean you get to have someone beautiful." The wind lifted the light material of her skirt from her legs and pressed it against her breasts. She was drunk already.

"Why do you stay with me," I said, and I was interested in what she'd answer.

"Because I can't stay away from you, of course," she said, and drooped on to me as if tranquil or exhausted or doomed, and the gold stained my chest. We lay still in the hungry sound of the waves and there was a burst of wings.

"It tried to get them," I said.

"Who?" Her face came up smudged and wan.

"Who else flies," I said. "They just wanted to sleep and it tried to get them."

"Stupid," she said, her voice slurred, "You asshole. It's the hot dogs, don't you know? They closed the shop." Then she turned away and was looking around for the bottle. Somehow it had gotten very far away, and I lay still, drunk also now, as she crossed me on all fours, got it, and drank. She sank down beside me where she would not rise in gold. Then I drank again and then it was empty. The waves crashed on, unwearied in their dream of life.

"Let's go," I said softly, and some birds screeched up.

"Flocks of them," she slurred.

"What?" I said.

"Crawling out of the waves," she said with exaggerated clearness.

"Let's go," I said standing up and holding out my hand. She got up and we walked across the sand. In a minute she was leaning again.

"You wouldn't let the whiskey man marry me," she said.

"You didn't want to marry him anyway," I said.

"Yes I did. You never want anyone else to marry me."

"Yes I do," I said, "It's you who won't."

"You're always lying. You say someone else instead of just saying yourself."

The lights on the highway hit us and we fell silent. The cars were like slaughtering waves.

We walked back to her room where in dark fields the maleos stalked.

9

I wake up and don't know who is sleeping beside me — reach cautiously — ah! — only a shadow. I float away, a darkness drifting within a greater darknesss.

Waz stoops by oasis pool. Lowering the veil, she turns away her face, where bright eyes glitter, and sings, though no sound comes through. The picture begins to fade. Colors and sounds pulsate back to whiteness and primal concord, contract to a chiming point of light, and vanish with a silvery peal. The long travail of the universe is ended. . .

I strive against the illusion and am awake, my eyes popping open. Morning, says a faint light, throbbing at the window, and I watch it. Grey fingers of that silent thief paw at the sill, reach up, and snatch the books on the upper shelves, then slipping along the wall grab what they will, and that is everything. Soon they get me too.

To sink, to desk, to door and shake it softly, back to desk. I sit in the chair breathing with open mouth, like an animal, and the day grows thick as thrown dust in the air. I feel it in the back of my neck, the shifting of the colors in that ageless dance we cannot see. I go to the window.

Outside my room autumn floods the branches with dying grandeur. Through the treetops that are wind-tossed like the waves I see Quintus dancing. His raggedy beard and hair float out in all colors. It is the dance of the yellow leaf, of the fading gold. Slowly he sinks in the billowing leaf-sea and is gone. Too late I am alert. Beneath his apparent simplicity he has danced a message, and I did not see it.

But yes it is too late for I hear night coming now, announced by far trumpets over treetops, that suzerain of shadows. Triumphant in drumfire the slow-marching stars glide in. They step more quietly and carefully than I do. It is plain that they too have something to hide. I turn away uneasily.

Sink door desk.

Why do I imagine that you love me? Though I can't even remember your name, which long ago I grew bored with and forgot... Gingerly I sit at the desk, and resist an impulse to turn on the light.

Sometimes, waking in the darkness, I have made up a voice for you, and words for it, and imagined you saying them to me, when the night grows deep and final...

But it is only the dark room, and I am alone. At my window is nothing so abstract and distant as a name...

Say — because of a good feeling I had once, lowering a glass to a table in a bar, and you were there. I close my eyes and sit unmoving in the dark.

Chairs scrape. A girl's voice floats in laughter with a clarinet. Around me the smoky bar comes up. Glasses clink above my desk. Someone's breasts float up and down by the jukebox, dancing. Names glitter like the bartender's smile, and change, and don't have to be true...

Laughing with foamy lips I lower a beer glass to a table...

But it is too free, too forgetful — already I feel it getting away. The doors are locked, the chairs are on the table, the bar is closed. The moon falls past my window...and oh when the moon falls, dearest, with an eagerness more evil than our dread, we rise up from our places and depart...

Come...

Outside the tavern door the street is dark, the air is still, the light is yellow and false and rare, on the separate ways that we walk home. In the alleys the night-roaming dogs work at the cans... Oh why do the bars ever close?! I turn on the light, the fan, and sit staring.

Now each, in his bright room, sensing the rats that move behind the veil, stills the hand from rending through the skull, the voice from shouting, Damn you! Who are you?! Damn you!

And many names come up, but I do not think that they are your name...

I lie down breathing hard and the blades of the fan turn too fast with their many breaths upon me. The engine starts, the bus roams hungry through the trees. There is silent laughter from an unseen throat. Teeth click and chatter as the rats work at the veil of thought.

Della! When I was a child I thought that if I knew your name I would know you. But now I have nothing so concrete and specific as a name. Only a song that never finds its key. Only a lonely wind wandering in a desert. Only black dreams where I fall through your hair as you walk in a gown of songs by an oasis where I cannot awaken.

I go to the window, but there is only my face again. Someone laughs from behind the glass my breath smudges. Painfully I still my flickering chest as the gaze veils over. Behind the glass the dark lady smiles in the waggling undulations of her dance. I reach and turn off the light.

Midnight, the dark says, throbbing at the window. And soon the starlight creeps in, all secret and silent, to see if it can find what I am hiding. And I lie back in the passionless embrace of that silent and secretive lover and float away, as Quintus falls past my window, his goofy robes trailing in the wind.

(Della, Della, listen to me now, if ever!
Where are you on your moth-boat flying, flying?
And have you yet no end of dying, dying?
Della, help! I am not very strong, or clever.)

10

Beneath the river, in the slime, I poked around. Then flippered back to the surface and drifted with the current past a hawklike man beneath a palm tree at a little oasis. From a window in a mud house a girl called, her face veiled with silk. Sun struck her hair. Rolling over, I drifted through murky dark. Turds floating past my face, I lay still among the reflections on the river.

The veil of waters rippled and, as if keeping some appointment, Quintus appeared, dancing in the dark suspension. Seeing me, he crooked a bony finger and led me into his golden room. He stared at me over the shining table, his hair and beard swaying gently in the currents.

"There is a place," he whispered, "where old men dance on the waves, old sailing captains and navigators and seers, whose rooms were swept out in an autumn weather, and books, and sing and dance on the tips of the laughing waves, like hair of a dancing girl in a smoky tavern, loops of her hair that float in the tuneful dark, lascivious dancing waves of the raw blue sea." His head wobbled, and he lapsed vacant and drooled. Then suddenly cried out again.

> "I pluck at Mago's skirts and he at mine
> Our whitened locks the girls of the waves entwine
> The wicked sweat beneath their apeskin flag
> And sail into the sea-king's murky bag.

> He pulls them down
> And then
> We old men clown
> Again
> Oh the dead have drunk a sweeter drink than wine."

He was gasping for breath and his face, formerly only vacant with idiocy, was now actually cross-eyed. He rose in a clumsy dance, singing the refrain again falsetto. "Oh the dead have drunk a sweeter drink than wine."

"Quintus," I said. "Why do you live under the river? Why do you have a golden room? Are you dead?"

He perched brightly on the table edge, beard flowing into his mouth, and gazed at me with bright eyes.

"There was a time," he cried gaily, "when the sea was young as you or I, my girl." He was so crazed I didn't try to stop him. "It lay palely shining in the untenanted room of the world, was glad in blueness, danced no sad or angry steps, as now, but lazy, gameful, young. Then something happened — hearts burned out, I think — came eery shadows of advancing dusk. We thought the waves which laugh forever here would give a face in stillness from the depths. Mad ones plummeted from cliffs around, showers of tortured blossoms on the waves. And ohh the strong bodies that floated with the fish," he clasped his wobbling head, "that sea-girls loved, though dead, within their caves." He swayed in the golden chair and came upright, old legs performing.

> "The body flowers gaily, it explodes
> In screaming bursts the burdened flesh unloads
> And ruined petals falling through the air
> Bleed on the tresses of the dancer's hair
> She pulls them down
> And then
> Swirls out her gown
> Again
> Our lives are flushed like shit down the commodes."

He danced wildly, as beneath an insufferable goad, yet wept out the refrain joyously, "Oh old men dance like trash down the commodes."

He collapsed in his chair and seemed tired. His head lolled on his chest, swaying with the currents that his dance had set going. In the silence some fish could be heard bumping the walls outside. The room seemed to glow more brightly, and I was afraid he would disappear without explaining anything.

"Quintus," I burbled, "who are you? Are you the god of this river, Quintus?"

He slumped lifelessly onto the table and I moved through the pale currents and touched his arm. Instantly his head floated up, eyes crossed and glittering, not looking at me. He whispered:

> "There is a way that brave men may swim deep
>   Cast from shipboard wailing in hot sun
>   Leaping in painful blossom from the bridge
>   Spreading the soul's dark petals like poor wings
>   Flutter and fall into the smoky den
>   Where drunk lascivious swivelling musky flanks
>   The cold sea goddess moves and down her neck
>   Our fingers fret the hooks and fret the darts
>   Untwine the galloon lace brocade and reach
>   Where gleam the chrysoprase carnelian
>   Sard jasper jacinth garnet heliotrope
>   And falling on her white breasts as she laughs
>   Tumble through the fingers of the waves
>   Till on the brutal floor in clement fire
>   The cold blooms chastened inornate severe
>   The sea-king's slattern girls shall pluck and wear."

He was weeping and cruel, rose staggering and waltzed toward me with outstretched arms.

> "The sea awaits with stanchless ravishment
>   The creatures of the other element

       Who placate, casting flowers for the dead
       Till all are looped about the dancer's head
       We pull them down
       And then
       They drown and drown
       Again
       Oh you will feel the sea-girls' blandishment."

The room glowed more brightly yet seemed to fade into an heraldic blackness. Quintus changed, his teeth gleaming sharp beneath huge flat eyes. Passing me by in a rush he danced out the door, lifting his old knees high.

And I paddled out to look for him at once, but there was only the garbage river again, cans and bottles and turds that the fish browsed lovingly.

             Why Quintus I have seen
             A dream you must have had
             Of what you might have been

             Why Quintus I am sad
             That someone was too strong
             And now your dreams are dead

             Old man! My lips have sung
             A song you must have known
             When gods were in your tongue

             Who came and hurt you then
             And made you feel you had
             To sing to the empty stone

             Why Quintus! I am sad

11

I wake up as the bus is entering a little station and get off in the clear morning light. It is a tropical town, with dogs, and natives of some kind, and open-air bars where I spend several days and nights, drinking and laughing with sleepy dark people who wear strange clothing. I trade my money for some kind with glowing heads on it.

During the day savages from the jungle come to town to trade cocoanuts and feathers for wicker-covered bottles of muscatel, or clothing, which means a bright red shirt, or knives. They stay for one night, get really drunk, then in the early morning when the sun, just up, tints the jungle both yellow and green, disappear into the trees, their faces glazed and satiated. Later in the morning the sun brings out only green from the leaves, and I sit drinking and gaze at it, watching the richness come through, then go home to sleep.

My room above a pin-ball parlor is sprinkled with the sound of tilting bells. I sleep with the fan swishing overhead till dinnertime or after, when the bells, which ring increasingly all evening, reaching by midnight a pitch of unremitting hysteria, wake me up. I shave and dress in their happy sound, humming, then go out.

By this hour the streets are full of my new acquaintances, and we wander from bar to bar with the night-roaming dogs, our friends, and finally fall down beside them, laughing, in the gutter. I have not told anyone my name and there is no need to. They call me Hey-hey or Jo-jo or anything that comes into their silly heads.

One night when wine has heated their poor brains to bubbling they demonstrate their trust in me by telling about those gods or jungle kings whose glowing heads are on their money. They assume that I, like others before me, have come to find secrets, make a map, and look for treasure. Endearingly, if incoherently, they jabber out the half-remembered tales. "Jo-jo, tellee you-you, me tellee you-jo." Then pull out a tattered bill and drunkenly point to the glowing heads.

I tell them I am not interested, all that is over for me now. I buy them more drinks and shake my head, pushing the money away, and try to distract them with some American songs which I am adapting to their kind of English. My lack of interest only goads them to ever greater efforts to interest me. Invariably, when the hour is late, someone slips up behind me, takes my arm, smiles to show what an honor this is, and begins: "Me-me, Jo-jo, tellee you-you," pulling out the bill with drunken dark hands, reeling. I cannot understand their stories, and end up asleep in a puddle of wine on the table.

In time they assume that my refusal to listen means that I want someone with greater authority. They drag the wild jungle traders to my room, half in awe of them themselves, where they strut around flashing knives and shrieking altogether unintelligibly, their dark heads glowing above the cheap red shirts. Soon all the jungle folk have heard of me. In the bars they stand at my elbow, silently staring.

Before long my evenings are ruined. They will give me no peace from their secrets, and I stay in my room longer each day, till the bells drive me out. Then I go out late by myself and wander the town with the dogs, my friends, drinking and laughing and singing by myself, and walk home at dawn, haggard and dirty, as the jungle folk watch and follow in little groups, always near.

One morning as I round the corner to my boarding house the proprietor of the pin-ball machines runs up in great excitement and jabbers at me all the way up stairs and to my door. I fall on the bed and try to sleep, but it's no use. I can't stop thinking of what he has said. The greatest honor of all, he explained, is coming to me, one which none of the townspeople has ever received. Some terrible jungle priest is coming to town with his followers, who are the ones with the knives, and will reveal the sacred places to me if he ascertains somehow that I am the one foretold in certain ancient prophecies.

I draw a bath and sit in the water and the news sweeps over me in a cold wave of tedium and resentment. I know how these things end. When I have shaved and dressed, I pack my few things, leave some money on the dresser, and set out for that corner where the bus loads or unloads on the rare days when anyone gets on or off here.

People dart out and pluck at my sleeve with hurt looks, grunting that I should not go. I pull away, shaking my head, and walk on. At the basket shop where the bus stops I buy cigarets and wine and sit on my suitcase outside as the natives gather, babbling like birds.

Morning passes and afternoon drags on. All day the red-shirted people slip in from the jungle to witness my meeting with the witch-doctor. There is a sullen tension in them when they realize that I am leaving. The sun goes down streaking the jungle with a look of blood. As night comes on, the red-shirted people swarm through the streets wild with whiskey. The day seems to have been incredibly long when at last the bus pulls up. I get on tired and nervous and wave halfheartedly from the window.

When we reach open country I breathe more easily and it occurs to me to ask another passenger what part of the world we are in. Tennessee, he says, just south of the Ozarks, and sure enough, soon we cross a little muddy river and come to the first hills.

12

[Baritone] *"My darling I have changed*
Since I began this book
I think I've caught the mange
My darling I have changed

Am I acting more deranged
Are there things I overlook
My darling I have changed
Since I began this book"

[Soprano] *"My darling you have changed*
Since I began this book
You are acting more deranged
My darling you have changed

Is your consciousness estranged
Is there madness in that look
My darling you have changed
Since I began this book"

Spring was turning into summer. I stood where the waves crashed, waiting for Della in the late afternoon.

And she was no longer just late. She wasn't coming.

She had flown through the crack in the vase.

Walking back to her place, I slept alone in her bed, waking from haunted sleep to the roars of the angel.

Days passed, then weeks.

Summer deepened and the afternoons grew full and cavernous, like deep breaths about to be exhaled. I walked down quiet avenues. Around me sunlight dripped from burgeoning elm and oak and climbed on the clustering blooms of the yellow-wood trees. Stillness of dusk, rich and frail as an eggshell of gold, stiffened each flower. The sound of a piano floated from a distant room and fell through a tree-hung window. The sun moaned its parting kiss above the waters.

I knocked on the doors of strangers, describing her half-coherently to people who shook their heads at once and were anxious for me to leave. My steps rang alone on the darkening avenues. Hot breezes hung like torn dreams in the blossoming trees.

I climbed the steps to Della's room and looked at the plastic curtains hanging still over the neatly made bed.

I slowed into an indefinite waiting like dying, describing her to doormen at hotels, old women at bus stops, and above all to the waves, which alone listened patiently and showed a just appreciation of the tale.

Night comes. I work the hypodermic with shaking hands. The blood leaps joyously into its little glass world. A pale mist, like the inside of a shell, flows over me. Quintus slides like a shadow into the wind-flaw of a puddle. Della laughs from the bathroom where the mole-buts are splashing. A terrible certainty takes me, that she is dead. Her reflection laughs from the water in the sink. An aureole of blankness ripples from white fur. Peering over the stairwell I see the reflection of her face as the scrubwoman leans and gazes into her pail. Before I can see it clearly she turns away.

I wake up covered with sweat in Della's bed. At once I sense something different about the room and yes there it is — an envelope thrust halfway under the door. I pick it up as in a dream and a little paper falls out:

> Suphis had a contempt for the gods
> and he composed the sacred book
> which I acquired in Egypt
> as being of great value.

For some time I cannot shake off the impression that her face is about to turn toward me.

> *So you're no fool, she says,*
> *No fool, I say, here's wine.*
> *And solemnly we praise*
> *The bright eternal vine.*

13

The water supply is drying up. I wash sparingly and inspect the slurry of durt stirred up in the sink. It floats into patterns and out and will take hours to settle. When it can no longer settle at all, it will be time to change it.

I sit at the desk and work for a little while at my list of wise men. Then I go to the window and the trees, green and gay, wave hello. *Hello,* I wave back. We are locked in a timeless greeting. Then I sit, my hair ruffled by the fan, smoking cigarets, and write more letters, most of which are thrown away. Soon the afternoon is tightening toward its end, and something is waving goodbye beneath the air.

Goodbye, goodbye.

I sit very still, breathing with open mouth, as late afternoon thickens the air around me like golden water.

I am going to tell it to you absolutely straight now.

I wanted to avoid the bullshit of the first part of this book. In moments of confidence I even hoped to correct it. So I went to the letters, thinking they would be truer than stories. But the lie was strong in me. And soon, to make the letters worthy of you and of me, I found myself lying in them too. And finally we were wrestling, I reading the words back and wondering if they were strong enough to take you. Crumpling the paper with a cry I would rise and pace the room.

(*Yes, afternoon is fading now... the sun touches my forehead with his parting kiss, torn from the gateway of all image.*)

Always I searched for you, on the lonely paths of the mind, casting my lines in the silvered streams for your name. But what I found were things not abstract and distant like a name — someone walking beside me who, somehow, is like me, on, I think, a beach, but possibly it is a dark meadow. I close my eyes and keep it dark, not to tempt myself. We are on a beach and there is dancing, there is a lyre of moonlight, a dancer on seven strings, a song. Or the meadow. And on a road nearby a car approaches. Only when it gets the best of me do I try to force the details to come clear. If it is the meadow, the car stops, goes dark. A figure crouches low in the darkness, possibly fixing a tire, but possibly not. Quickly other things stream in, trying to adulterate the memory, trying to make it an imagining. The beach, and a face is forming over the water; there is laughter, there is emptiness, there is light. The car, and we drive all night, you lying in dark tangles of hair by the door. The beach, and someone is rising, someone is dancing, the moon — I see doors opening everywhere, but it is never your door — figures slip from the back seat and rush toward us — the headlights flicker on, wax full on your screaming face — I stagger up — your face! your face! I lurch about the room, knocking things to the floor, gasping as a picture tries to form on the bright still page.

It is only after struggling for hours with the riot in my mind that I get back to the thin stream of memories that I know are pure in themselves, however faded, and which will someday bring back the rest.

(*It is darkening swiftly now, leaves waving goodbye goodbye.*)

And then the question arose whether the letters must be purified also. So I went to the songs. And yes they were more truthful — but that was because they named no names, said nothing in so many words.

(*Night is creeping close now, brushing softly at the window.*)

But something must be said, I thought, because the characters in my book still are clawing at the veil. How pitifully they gasp for final rest!

(*I lean among colors that the dark has muted into friendly purity now, the red green gold like muted trumpets from the forest.*)

Finally I had to give something to the postman, to prove that you were real. I would kneel, in a silence full of tears, and pull the crumpled sheets from the wastebasket, smoothing them for the envelope. . .

On seven strings

I rise from the wastebasket, smoothing this page, and go to the sink and yes they are dancing freely still, they cannot rest now, it is time. I pull the plug and watch as they drift out waving goodbye.
Goodbye, Goodbye.

the dancer sings

The light is falling like a hectic golden grease over my hand and the paper now, and soon I will write it out fine and true.

and leaps before

When was it that I realized I could say anything in the letters, anything at all?

the burning door

When did I realize, with a rush of pain and gladness, that they would never be answered?

Evagrius Ponticus
Who taught
The invulnerability
Of the flesh

14

"Dearest honey I've been told
  That your hair is running gold
  That your shoulders and sweet bosom
  Glow with gold beyond all reason
  And yes I've seen it, hoarded up,
  Finest wine from sweetest cup
  Flowing over lips and chin
  Cleansing molten streams within
  Purging out the fire and heat
  Vomiting disgorging it

"Sweetest darling I've been told
  That your love is purest gold
  That it cleans and honors me
  Makes me what a man should be
  Drinking health in generous measure
  From that richest purse of pleasure
  Your sweet mouth unmixed with pain
  Can you then my dear explain
  Why strangling burned and stained I lie
  Upon your golden flesh to die"

I walked, hands in pockets, along the tideline, among the shells and crumpled sea-things that washed up, till night came on and stirred the waters to unsatisfied moaning. The sweet scent of garbage was carried off by the faintest of breezes. I lay down on the sand and closed my eyes and a kind of despair settled over me. Della was like one of those most gentle breezes that leap so lightly over the treetops and are gone. She had brushed against me and I had been unable to hold her. The lovers walking in the moonlight seemed both beautiful and tragic. They still had the brightness of life upon them, the gold which is past all counting. It had fallen away from me. I was being cleansed in the darkness, yet dying. I began to drift to sleep. As always Quintus waited for me behind some veil, took me by the hand, and beckoned me into the darkness.

I saw a betusked bewhiskered form, flippers raised in horrible benediction, about to pull shut his robe of whiteness around her.

The sink dripped like a tolling bell.

Past the whiskey man's store in the late moonlight I ran, past Easy's Place where old wine stained the steps. At the hotdog stand I heard them inside, sprouting little brown wings and trying to get used to them, flopping around in the mustard and things.

I stumbled into the stinking hallway and felt my way up the stairs. With shaking hand I grasped the doorknob, pushed it easily past the broken lock, and stepped in.

Something like silver was coming through the windows; the little dying plant was a dusty silver green. I leaned back on the door and closed my eyes where little suns glinted and died, dreading to see the dust gleam flat on her empty bed, the rusty sprung coils, the moonlight dripping to the floor.

Then I heard the little laugh, as necessary and sufficient as the key that turns in the lock, and looked, and she lay, alone, in the bed of dusty silver, gleaming dimly, like a moon strangling in winter clouds, or a salamander glowing through ashes. Bright as sunlit water her hair flowed down to the pillow. And almost before I had sobbed aloud in the full rush of joy — but not before — came the nightmarish familiar other voice, and I saw him stretched out on the floor like a dog beside her bed, his eyes gleaming coldly as his tusked mouth twitched.

Della, dead girl, fallen dancer... You are a silent moth over me, truly you are. I wake in the evening when the papers rustle with breezes, and you are there. We are in your mother's house and she is gone. We walk through the rooms in cool evening, sit on the chairs, the beds, watching the night come, serene.

And always when I go wrong you cut in through the iceberg of my brain with your little hatchet that does not hurt, reminding me with very little pain, "Dreams are light, dreams are gay, dreams are airy things to make us free."

And I straighten out, Della, really I do. I stir on the cot, blinking happily, like a fly, and smile as your moth wings flutter near. You float over in the sky, changing always, and remind me that I am happy.

Not so, not so, all things. All other things torment me, Della, pretending they are not you. I kiss a mouth at a party and it is yours. An old man raves of princesses, and are they also you, Della?

Pitying myself, I grow peevish and think that I never knew you. But you only laugh and say, "Silly boy! You knew me once. I just went away." Oh Della! What did you do then? Where did you go? "I got cold. So I turned on the stove. I lay pressed against the floor. And many baskets would not hold me. Somewhere a flute was playing as I sailed away on a night-ship. And I talk to you, just you, forever now. Because I want you to be happy too." Oh but I am not Della. I still am so hungry. And the water is dirty with old men. And every mouth I kiss is so sweet. And beside your bed, your bed which floats away, there is a beast with bright eyes, and I must conquer him.

15

(Yes Della honey I'll be there
When morning's yellow in the air
To sweep the floor and take the garbage out

And when you're lying in the bed
I'll kneel beside your golden head
And tend the little fires you forgot

Oh Della I will be your friend
Until I will not say the end
To pull the shades and break the final lease

And when it all is over dear
I'll still be here I'll still be here
To scrub away that little spot of grease)

The wind blew her scarf and it bobbed as in obeisance to the sun. The day was warm and we were stoned. The music of a carousel came through the trees.

"This zoo has no animals," she complained.

"There they are," I said, and we sat on a bench where little squirrels gathered in a polite circle around us, squirming teeth and noses in the sun-shot air. "They'll bite my hand," she whined, holding the popcorn.

"Just pour it out on your lap and sit still," I said.

"Why would I want them in my lap," she said. She looked at me and I became lost in the images which refracted and multiplied in her eyes.

A zookeeper appeared from nowhere, smiling like a child's nightmare of cops, and said, "Enjoying yourselves?"

"Oh yes indeed," I answered. "Very nice animals you have here. Although these squirrels are the only ones we have found so far."

"Those are zizels," he replied, speaking with that exaggerated clearness now, "and this is a zoo. And you cannot feed them." He arched an eyebrow sternly at Della. "The exit, through which you just entered, is over there. You are now in the Z section. If you wish, you may feed the ziczac, or the zho, or the zimb, an Abyssinian insect which eats only blood and waits in that little house." Della managed a nod of agreement and he sidled off, smiling wanly.

"He's not really going away, you know," she said.

"I know," I said. "He's stopping by that water fountain and in a minute he's going to look back because he knows you'll feed those zizels again as soon as you think he's gone.

"But the great thing is," I continued, staring deep into the deepness of her eyes, "that they've got a zimb." She was rooting in the popcorn box sullenly.

"He just wants to eat off my lap too," she said.

"You really think everyone does, don't you," I said.

"Not everyone," she said primly, already feeding the zizels again, but I knew she was lying. And I knew she was right, everyone did, and that made me mad.

'Fuck those zizels," I said. "The zizelkeeper is coming back."

"Fuck *him*," she said, and now he was mad too because he heard us saying bad words in his zoo.

I pulled her over to the zeber's cage and she began feeding him handfuls because she knew he was probably unfeedable too. I found the sign and sure enough he was though you couldn't tell why to look at him. There were two of them watching us now and one of them had a gun.

"My dear," I said softly, "I've got about an ounce of heroin on me and if you get us busted I will rip every hair from your fucking head. I will bald you." I grabbed the box from her hand.

Her face got brittle and sort of separated into parts. "Stop it," she said shrilly. "Do you think I need you to run me?" She stalked into the Y section like I was beneath contempt and I followed, eating some popcorn. We had started at the Z's and were only at the Y's and it was going bad already. We walked along in silence. Then we saw the sign that said, YABOO RIDE.

She leaned on the fence, her breasts pressed against the rail. "Why do they call that pony a yaboo?" she asked. I shrugged. But it was a neat little pony. She got on among children and I took the reins. We walked along the bridle path where the air hung green and still and Chinese monkeys smiled from the branches of overhanging trees.

"I want this yaboo to run," she said.

"I know," I said, "but he might need an injection. The withers is the best place." We were behind the W section now. I patted the yaboo experimentally and he looked at me with runny eyes.

"What do they keep here," she said, "wombats?"

"Uh-uh," I said.

"How do *you* know?"

I stopped and stroked the yaboo's hairy face. "This is where they keep the walruses," I said. "Nothing can make them run. This is where *you* live."

"Stop it," she said. She looked straight ahead and prodded the yaboo with her heels. "Come *on*," she said. "What are you holding him for?"

I stuck one finger up the yaboo's nose experimentally.

"He needs an injection," I said. "You can tell from the nose." I let him go and he walked along slowly, glancing back at me while her heels kicked hard. "Actually," I said walking, "they're getting rid of the walruses here too. They're going to shoot at them and see if that makes them move. Of course they know it won't. But then they can say it was a mistake. In case the SPCA complains."

"Will you stop it," she said. "What the fuck do you want." Her heels were kicking continuously. "Damnit," she said. "It won't *move*." This yaboo wouldn't eat off her lap.

"If you don't get rid of that walrus," I said, pulling his lips up and feeling his teeth, "I will."

"Stop it," she shouted. "He hasn't done anything."

"It's not him" I said, "it's you." I held the yaboo by his tongue, experimentally.

"What's the matter," she shouted, her voice rising to flight in known territory, "are you jealous?"

"Yes," I shouted, just to keep from shouting no, and looked at her. "Get *rid* of him."

"Damn you," she screamed, her voice gone now, as I slid my whole hand into the yaboo's soft hot mouth. "Shit! Goddamn you! Don't you think I've *tried?*" We were behind the T section and the keepers were speaking Tupi, a Brazilian Indian language. They turned and looked at her flushed angry face. She was all screaming and glaring. The yaboo was all tressy and tousy.

"Like hell," I said. Then, "Tilly-vally! This yaboo can run."

I gave him his injection while the tinnamour watched sadly from his cage.

"Why then," she screamed, "you smart-ass, why didn't I then." The tittle-bat was grinning toothily as if enjoying a domestic comedy. I pulled the needle out and slapped the yaboo hard. He leapt into flight and I scrambled up behind her and took the reins. A lion roared through the sun-shot leaves.

"Because he'll make you a lousy slob like he is," I shouted, "and that's what you want, isn't it, to be a lousy slob that only the SPCA cares about." She was gasping and her yellow hair flew back in my face. The tittup of the yaboo's heels was loud and clear.

"You don't care a damn about him," I shouted. The lion roared gold rage and the yaboo raced rejoicing in his new ringing hooves.

She was crying and her yellow hair flew back in my face.

The yaboo ran tantivy-tantivy through the T section, faster than he had ever dreamed he could go.

> (*Feel the deep undertow*
> *Of sea round the jetty*
> *We'll have a bungalow*
> *Oh the deep undertow*)

Oh feel the joy that grows in the high room! Like a lonely planet it wings round a distant sun. Pure and free, it berserks its way through time. Feeding on secret light, it grows rank, sprouts musky vegetation, fecundates.

I go the the window, breathing the electric dark.

"Goodbye," I cry, waving to the stars as we tear out of orbit and steer for the far off galaxies. Tears press at my eyes. A new star sign is born. A new life need and a new way of satisfying it. I switch on the fan and sit in breezes never felt before. There on the desk is my little friend, my pen, that dapper, atomy, pocket-size, elfin fellow. He waits, while I work at the knots.

Memory is hard, I say. It stands up angry, goes out walking, and is gone. Sits plump and gracious in its chair again, smiling and gesturing, paternal and kind. Slowly the knot unwinds, deep inside.

There is a clatter of hoofbeats at the window — trees flash by — I remember — the seventeenth degree of Gemini and that eminent star the Bull's Horn attaining it amid plague and fire — the fixed stars turning in their cold preciosity — ice hanging from the eaves — the blacksmith playing a tune on a cornet as snow settles down... I lean closer and still my breath. She kneels by oasis pool, rises, begins to turn... I remember — a promise, yes of that much I am sure — but why was it not kept? Oh but of course; it was not a promise made to us but one we made. And those of us who did not keep it had to wander. But why did we not keep it? Was it only a gallant song, and the very gallantry of making it the reward? Yes yes that must be it. And if so then made to a lady, and if to a lady then made for the fling of her scarf as she descended from horseback on a windy day — for her lips eyes lips and their smile — oh all our hearts caught stunned in that flying gauze — for that moment when she would not withdraw her eyes though they gazed on my naked heart leaping. I stare more deeply into the darkness. She rises and sits enthroned beside the water. Will she strip off the veils and descend into the pool — or has she ascended from it, dripping bright foam? I remember — a promise — no — a song — why did I say a promise? — and those of us who did not hear it had to wander. But that wasn't fair! Perhaps an old beggar man hummed it in the alley by the cans and froze to death before morning. Or the blacksmith tapped it on cushioned stops in the snowy courtyard in the dark and the shutters were tight. While I waited on my lady in her chamber. Or perhaps — yes that must be it — perhaps we sang it ourselves — yes, I remember now — we were foolish and young and sang the wrong words to an old song — words we had made up in secret perversity and perhaps believed were true — . . . but some king got angry. Oh! It was so unfair! I lie down beneath the fan. My heart is like slaughtering waves.

You are killing me and I don't even know your name.

From the darkness I hear a little sound where on her dress birds thrash in nets of stitching. I turn and see her dimly, enthroned in my chair, beside my desk, in the darkness. Her hands arms hands their invitations — I should turn on the light now. Suddenly my hands are full of her white breasts, huge, squirming liquid soft in my fingers — her tongue is hot — her hair drifts golden — she sobs with desire — I drive it into her place of moans and screams and my room fills with howling — her weeping song rains down and at last she sleeps. . . . She breathes quickly beside me, then more slowly, then is still.

I rise and go to the window, lighting a cigaret. There is a tiny tiny movement in the walls. Outside, the moonlight is leaping with silver steps through the leaves. It stretches before me like a net or an invitation, and I turn away.

I lie down and smoke in the darkness and her face hovers over me in the watery moonlight. I remember the blacksmith shuffling his feet in the courtyard, tapping a tune on the bent horn held in rags, snowflakes settling on his head, shoulders, hands. Her hair crawls onto my shoulder with a touch that is irritating, even sinister. Suddenly I become one with some dark color and cannot be distinguished from it.

Now I am going to tell you about sleep.

There is a darkness in which I hear only your name. A box of Greek words. A king. At his feet, like wattles of a fowl, the tunes of dances turning in the dust. Behind a still bronze door waits someone whom we cannot see.

I wake in darkness, tingling with nervous fear, and light a cigaret. Why is there always a king, waiting in a country of dark, clothed in the patchwork of dreams? Della turns and I am electrified by her touch. Her hair floods the pillow with rivers of hidden gold. Waking fitfully on the floor beside the bed, Wally tries to sing. A sort of honking bark comes out. Many times he reaches for the bed with flippered arm and falls back. His hideous song of love is unwelcome here. I wake up —. No. Sleep more deeply yet. Over the desert sand a song comes from the oasis. Della is singing there in the dunes her song of stained gold as the moon wanders over, Wally his song of lust and guilt, of wronged women... A plaintive duet. What weighs on my heart so heavy, so heavy? I raise my head from a pool of blood on the pillow. Who is that shuffling through the door which should not be opened? I am staggering blindly and do not remember getting up.

I turn on the light, go where Wally lies slumped beside the dresser and drag him by the hair acoss the room as he screams. Della wakes and shouts at me from the bed.

"What are you doing? Leave him alone! What's the matter with you?"

His hair rips out and I drag him by his flailing arms and legs. "Getting this motherfucker *out* of here," I shout. She gets up naked and struggles with me on the floor. I throw her off again and again and drag him out. I had forgotten how much I hated him. The joy of it is so great that I hurl him through the bannister, breaking it, and he falls with horrible screams and crashes below, in a little while gets up and goes.

Della is off her root, wailing and clawing at me. I throw her onto the bed. "Taking no shit from you either," I shout. But she keeps coming back, her breasts shaking as she screams toward the door. I get the hypodermic ready but am afraid of breaking off a needle in her, and put it away. All night she pretends to sleep, then rises for the door when she thinks I am dozing.

When at last morning swims through the window like a hungry grey fish she is asleep, her golden hair tangled in hot sad threads around her face. I kneel and with lightest of touches, reverently, pull it away from her nose and mouth.

When I raise my arms the papers are wet with perspiration. I try to smooth them but it won't work, they are curled for good now. I add a name to my list and lie down to sleep as the moon sets.

Sonchis the Saite
who knew
the kingdoms beneath
the sea.

16

The old songs we have played too long
Will play no longer, sing no more,
On seven strings the dancer sings
And leaps upon the bestial floor

. . . it is morning and the sun floats distantly over the forest. The leaves and I are lost in a dream of light.

Della sings in greyness on the bed, her hair like clusters of yellow blossoms in the gloom. I lie still and listen to her morning song, that song of grief. Then we rise, walk to the shore, and swim, slow and dazed, beneath the sun's intolerable splendor.

Suddenly, as I turn away from the window, the sound of the flicking fan blades frightens me.

I look it up.

"Mercury rising to the airy triplicity: great and high winds, and very hurtful."

I turn back to my work, fishing in the deep streams of the mind.

Through the long afternoons we swim in the lake, wander the still sand shores, make love in the insolent boat of her bed that can stand all burnings, and I am immensely happy. That is too weak.

(I go to the window. Evening, that puppetmaster of dreams, is summoning his shadows to the forest now.)

Suppose you leapt from the tree limbs and knew you could fly; knew that you would lie broken on the hard earth when it caught you — but until then you could fly, could fly. . .

(Night, that gentle choreographer, is leading his dancers to my window now.)

I turn back to the darkened room and he is there, he is sitting there clearly now, his back hunched like mine, a sad king dying in a darkened throne room. . . The box of Greek words lies flung away on the floor. . . His shadowed face is staring through or past me, at some other whom I cannot see. His voice, thick with pain, drips brights words in the air.

"Oh wise man, singer of dreams, behind whose head stars crash in pretty dances, their captains steering as you play in paths of death. . ." He is staggering in pain or rapture, cries out. "Thou master of the storms of the strings, oh lover of their taut strung gleams. . .

> "Sing of your favorite's hair
> How it gleams with a clement fire
> Of her eyes, how they tell no lies
> Of her lips, and her fingertips
> Of her breast, your sweet place of rest
> And her hands — tell of love's commands. . ."

Somewhere a million stars careen on collision courses, but our lord, that bold tyrant, Polycrates, does not deign to turn to the frantic astrologers. Careless of the fate of worlds he lies still in the wash of songs, face flushed, hands clenched in exaltation round the cup. His heart is tangled in the seven strings. . .

Sound of a trunk lid closing — a screech of tires in the alley — lights rove over the wall, fix on him — he is gone.

At the window I see that the moon has risen, dancing over the wave-tops of the trees. Soon Venus follows, and I watch her, wending her bright way over the ages. The plot thickens as the night heats up. Neptune strides quickly into Libra, and Uranus, the spiteful and contentious father, steers for the tropical sign in a baleful boat with dark sails. . . What does he want there? His lips part and a laughter like death slides out.

I sit down on the cot. What weighs on my heart so heavy, so heavy?

We wade in the lapping waves and swim past the tumbled boulders, diving and surfacing like creatures of dream, or strayed beasts from the far caves below.

Summer rises to his glaring empyrean, scattering hysterical yellow promises over field and city. We fuck in a furious cold, two reflections of match flames trying to be one.

Then one day something is new in the heat — a fever that breaks into a yellow cry — she crawls from the water on all fours and looks about strangely, remembering nothing. And I take her, sleek and soft, to my chest, and kiss her in the dream, not caring.

"Venus decumbent: sunstroke, puking fevers, pulsatilla."

I discover a critical opposition coming, Uranus in Cancer and Neptune in Capricorn, and dash off a note to the papers: "There will be famine in India, civil strife in North Africa. . ." The pig-men come with their robes of stars and impaling stakes, but I stand silent by the window and in time they leave.

She crawls onto me, slopping her breasts on my face like slopping waves, wheels slowly, like a cow in a stall, and sucks at my cock, her head rising and falling wetly, ruminatively, tongue etching language of serpents on my spine.

I look it up.

"Venus at midheaven: dancing; gold and silver; skill at chess."

I finger her hot cunt, then topple her slowly, like a great tree falling, climb on, and fuck her for hours, aiming and shooting in all directions against her silken walls. . .

"Venus under the moon: shipwrecks; abundance of water; snow in the spring."

She kisses me slowly slothfully thoughtfully all over, covers me with wine and licks it off with an abiding thirst. She fills her mouth from the bottle and blows me, drinking wine and come together in sweet choking swallows.

"Trouble from the sea; a star, her hair blown by the wind."

I ride her this way and that, fucking deep into cunt mouth ass every valley and nerve, seeking in first one room of her inner mansion then another. She comes for hours without pause, lying on a bare wire of the universe. The room drips with cries that well up from the abyss at the heart of being.

"Kings will break leagues and compacts; hailstorms; detriment to women."

She falls slowly through light thick as water, her breasts sliding smooth as mucous through the foam...

"*Death of the queen; star chaplet falls; helianthus.*"

I go to the window.

And when you sailed out on the night-ship, Della, when you turned on the gas and lay pressed against the floor, then did you find what you wanted? "I didn't want anything, dearest; you don't understand yet. I didn't want anything at all. And now I float like a cloud, change like a dream, tangle like a skein of words, and the baskets of people's hearts can hold me, if they want, and I will still be free." *The water rolls away from her like congealed light; her shoulders and hips rise from it like universes exploding.*

"I want this yaboo to run," she said. And we stung it with the zimb and rode away o so fast to the land where marascas grow.

And many baskets would not hold them...

> Oh tap the buttons fast
> Dream singer, this can't last
> Sweet pleasure has an angel that rebukes
> Outside the door he lies
> With unmelodious eyes
> That gleam like dogs' and flash like filthy jokes.

I ride on. It is night, morning, night. Rain splashes at the windows. Some seasonal change sets in. I get off the bus at the edge of a swamp with no town in sight and walk down a little dirt road. There is intermittent shade where the vines and moss hang low. At a ramshackle bayou store which the swamp dwellers approach in boats I buy a Panama hat, wander out on the porch lighting a cigar, and see an unpainted window-broken houseboat half pulled on to the bank.

I rent it from the storekeeper and push off into the swamp, poling into the maze of sunlit corridors.

I stand at the window and gaze at the stars as they turn forever and ever in desire for rest.

No rest, no rest, and tortured memories like old dreams. The arena of volence stretching far and far... The bleared stars its bloodied sands...

17

> (Oh do not be in too great haste
> To pull the bell that stops the bus,
> That says, "It's through, the race is raced,
> There's nothing left here now for us
> All time moves, and ours has passed...")

Somebody is calling me loudly, insistently. I stagger from the cot, half asleep, and my hand is on the door knob when I realize that it is coughing and it is coming from me. I lean retching over the sink. When the fit passes, I turn on the light and look it up.

"If Venus be afflicted by Saturn, consumption and catarrh will be very fatal."

That is not reassuring. No, not reassuring at all. Still, looking farther, I find, "If by Mars, then smallpox and murderous outrages will cause great mortality." And hence it seems my cough, while unpleasant in itself, may be insurance against murderous outrages... And that would be reassuring; yes, very reassuring indeed. I must learn to live with it...

I try to turn off the fan, twisting and pushing various knobby protuberances on it, but each time that awful swinging head comes round my hand leaps back in fright.

I turn back to my work.

The pages look unfamiliar. But that is understandable.

The images of memory are unclear, I say, for the closer the heart comes to its desire, the less can the memory follow it. And the less the memory has followed, the more will the heart, on returning, deceive with its lying tales...

Strangely, at this moment I remember that the fan can also be stopped by unplugging it, and laying down my pen I follow the cord over table edge, around chair legs, across the floor, and — it goes out under the door. I can feel my heart beat. For the first time I realize that I have forgotten whose room that is out there. I sit on the splintery floor and breathe loudly. Finally I edge over to the door, shake the knob lightly, and lay my ear against the wood.

Is that a footstep in the hallway? Is that a key turning? A mattress squeaking?

I hold my breath and have a strong impression that the door is about to open which for some reason I feel should not be opened. I have a strong impression that Quintus will lean in and smile, gesturing as if to invite me out with him or perhaps to introduce me to someone who is with him.

I tip-toe away from the door and look it up.

"*Mars in the house of the moon: inventions; transmigration of princes; disasters on railways.*"

Disasters on railways!?

And what of buses?!

I turn back to my work, fishing in the deep streams of the mind.

One must work with these images (O my love) not, at first, with high purpose, as if to determine what they mean — but humbly. Like a child digging for things hidden in the sand. . . Simply to find out what they are.

Is this only an ancient joke, dropped through a laughing fissure of some brain long dead? No matter. We put the pieces together and, walking out to the edge of the diaphanum, hurl the rag ends as hooks or nets into the abyss, if perhaps some wandering image may be pulled clamoring from the deep, squirming and flashing in the net. And thus we labor over all the terrain of the soul. . . Working outward toward that final wall behind which, we imagine, something waits, at the center of it all. . .

I imagine there is someone waiting in the hallway, quietly clearing his throat. Then I imagine there is not.

And when the remembered world fades out, the nets haul in empty, the abyss is still — then one must torment the brain like a greedy and deceitful servant and pursue its wounded cries into the dark. Might not (one must ask) (o my dear) might not some part of that which was merely imagined, merely mused as a worthless joke in melancholy, or even dreamed in deepest sleep, some fragment which wandered loose over ontological seas for untold aeons before washing up on a shore of the unconscious brain . . . be true? And be used to fill out the picture?

I stand up quickly and as quickly sit down.

But here the mind and its desperate ambitions rub shoulders with a yet darker world, and recourse must be had to other repositories of past fact than memory — such as the stars, the suspicious coincidences of song and language, and the falling waves.

If king, for example, rhyme with sing, here are suspicions enough. Is there a music man, some tambourine beggar with a hurdy-gurdy, who sits a throne not his, far in the galactic night? Having slain the true king with — a bent horn perhaps? Swung from behind a turning door?

Yes, here are suspicions enough!

And more than enough, surely, when we proceed to observe that song rhymes with wrong (the falseness of that king), and with strong (a hoodlum or bully), prong (a weapon), thong (with which he has bound the shrieking lord), bong, dong, and gong (all sounds of violent blows or of inaugural processions), throng (a band of insurrectionists, or a people unruly from false governing) — and with very few other words of the same length, yes, very few indeed!

Here is suspicion that rises near to certainty! And what have the stars to say of this?

I look it up.

"If Jupiter (the planet of kings) be afflicted in Sagittarius (the house of song) there is much danger of the decease of the reigning monarch."

Indeed! And further:

"If Mercury (the planet of song and beggary) be Lord of the Year, and Mars (the significator of armed law) be afflicted by him, women will have their throats cut and some will be mutilated by experts; criminals will give a great deal of trouble. In short, murderous outrages will be apalling!"

Murderous outrages!

There is a pounding at my door! I am up and the chair is falling.

I remember! I remember! Her hair like a rush of words down her shoulder — murderous outrages and the box of Greek words flung away in a petulant rage — the dizzy dark through which I staggered to the window, the shutters crashing open to cold air and the raggedy shuffle of that murderous fiend as he advanced through the courtyard tapping a tune on the cornet in the dusk. She rises from the chair, waves breaking like folds of light about her face — there is a step — a dragging step from the seafloor — coming closer in the hallway — a hand rises to the door which should not be opened —

    I still my moaning breath and lay my ear against the wood — ahh, faintly now . . . there it is. . . The slow persistent chipping of a tooth . . . a breath so small, so light, so unconcerned. . . Whose is it? I cannot remember. Surely this is what the Arabs called the Criminals' Holiday, when those wild singers, who would sing their own song — who would sing no other — will rise in clamorous affray from the fishy shore. . . My feet are slipping in muck. Why the fishy shore? I cannot remember. Did the Arabs say that? I go down on all fours in the slime. Probably I meant the dishy chore, since such men could get no jobs save as dishwashers. Yes that must be it. I gather the strips of wet paper with shaking hands. Or wish-no-more, signifying the gratification of their desires at last. Yes that is it.

    I look at the door and a whiteness foams over my eyes. Now not one but two black cords disappear beneath it. I make a little sound. Suddenly I realize that the bus is moving very fast, much faster than it used to I think, crashing through the tree limbs with a strange crippled motion. Della turns in her sleep and I am electrified by her touch. I force myself not to scream. Two little burned black bodies, twisted around each other, writhing in electrical fire to another world. Her hair crawls like golden spiders onto my shoulder. I follow it with my eyes, squatting by the sink, and yes this one goes to the light.

    So they have my light now too! I sit back in amazement.

    No this is not reassuring at all.

That king, I fear, was much maddened by darkness. Else why did he rise and kick the box of Greek words, send language flying like a broken face? No, not reassuring. I thrust, for an instant, my fingertips under the door, then snatch them back. And I can feel that someone else has looked at them. And, yes, if I hold my breath now she stops hers too. And when I crouch and raise my nose and sniff I can smell her in the air, pungent of iron and sweet as the lilac spray...

"*Mania and epilepsy; a scorpion gripping the moon; the expectoration of blood...*"

I open the dry paper to spread it under the sink, and a news item catches my eye.

"In Cracow an astrologer has proclaimed a new zodiac that bears no relation to the known skies." I spread it on my desk beneath the light and lean close. "When asked why he did it, at first he tried to get sympathy, saying, 'Because I was lonely,' but when pressed, and when it became clear that he would be punished anyway, he admitted that it was because he feared death..."

"*Strangers in the doorway; an autumn wind...*"

Morning rises to stunned gold perfection on the peaks of the city, threatening to hurl them down with dizzy heat.

Della rises like a tired dancer who no longer cares what the audience thinks.

We walk through late summer haze, mad howls of machines, slow wash of dying songs from Easy's records...

Slowly I sit back and light a cigaret.

I suppose it's true that we're all going to die. But it's sort of hard to believe.

Della is dying. She has bad habits and can't cure them. Wally, well, he might as well be dead for all the difference it makes. But he'll probably live a long time... Quintus died, I think... And those others — I'll try to explain about them later... There's so much guilt in this job...

I wonder if everything that happens to the characters in my book is my fault.

I paste the article about my colleague from Cracow in my scrapbook and sit smoking. Saturn is the hateful one, really, lurking in hidden paths, then dropping from the branches with a hoarse shout when you least expect it...

Della unzips my pants and my cock rises hungrily and grows huge, waves like a candleflame before her hypnotized face, then spills molten gold as she lifts her hot reaching box down over it for the benediction.

I wonder idly if it is a trap.

Finally I write cautiously, asking only to begin a correspondence if he is so disposed, and not committing myself on any of the questions facing either him or me. Sealing the envelope I go to the door and stare at the whorls and labyrinths that meander endlessly back and forth in the wood. I still my breath. Whose room is that out there? Fear closes on my heart and I can hear my breathing. Tears dim my eyes. I try not to believe that there isn't anything out there at all.

For where would you be, my beloved, if not outside there gnawing to get in?

I turn like a little beast in a trap and discover to my amazement that outside the window it is a bright afternoon. The leaves wave greenly. The squirrels leap gaily. The birds sing freely. (*Hello!*) And suddenly I am sure that it is Quintus who is doing this to me — because of a slight which he received long ago and which was richly deserved anyway. Alright. Let him torment me. The bastard. He is trying to show me your face, which I work at reconstructing all day long. But he would show me something that I know could not be you, something that I do not want to see. At least I can keep him out of my list of great men, I can still do that and he knows it, he resents it, he can't stand that.

And at first, as I gaze at that bright tissue on my wall, it seems less sinister that Quintus comes for me in the daytime, but, upon reflection, more. For if it is daytime it seems less likely to be only a dream. And between being confused by yet another dream (which is bad enough) and being threatened with actual murderous outrages in the afternoon — I would choose the former.

*(Epimenides of Phaestos
purified the city of most luctual plague
asked as payment only
a shoot of the sacred tree.)*

(And so we stamped our feet in the cold behind the stable and agreed. There would be new words, new songs. We had lain in the lap of the rich like stitched birds, fattening their ugly daughters with songs of hypocrisy, the fat arms swinging, faces preening, to the titting and the tatting of the flattering lies of the tunes. And now there must be new ones, songs cold like the snow and hot like the stamping foot; songs like a veil of words for the dark lady. Songs like the strings of ice that the stars shoot from their eyes.

(Then the hoofbeats, a clattering and chattering, dark shoes, and we cried,

> Oh, soft, thou bed of snow,
> Do not betray us so
> Be still, thou stern-eyed owl
> The night is not yet full,

and crouched behind the stables while they clattered about with a jingling of steel implements, and I knew who had betrayed us, his feet like dull fat clubs in bags of wrapping shuffle, chill clubs of fingers tapping buttons of lying music and the shutters of my lady's windows darkened while a king's mouth moans of ancestral lineaments. In the darkened throne room he sits stung to mad brooding, about his feet the tunes of dances twining in the dust.

(I remember the tapping of cushioned stops coming closer in the corridor as I play for my lady on the clarinet, dancing on my dainty feet. An evil planet in the eighth house afflicting the moon. A broken face reeling down from heaven. A city fallen to no purpose, because some radiant star poured spent gold from its mouth.

(Some trumpeter pressed the buttons of his horn and we marched off, over the desert, with the gay tunes in our hearts, the songs of stained gold and wronged women. . .)

Far off in the sky the wind cries hello.

("Sunlight in golden hair; leaves on the wind; a burning door.")

18

My god I brought my heart out for you Della
And made it build a world where there was nothing
I set my life to singing a capella
My breath I made a song for our betrothing

But you went speeding toward some martyrdom
And when you crashed I could not call the wrecker
And when we kissed your mouth was cold and numb
A bit of foam upon a toppling breaker.

"Suphis had a contempt for the gods," I read, "and he composed the sacred book which I acquired in Egypt as being of great value." I tendered her the note. "What do you think it means," I said. We walked through burning streets toward the shore.

The drug clicked her eye lenses open when we entered the shade and screwed them down when we emerged. Closed slyly now, they turned, slowly smiling. "An advertisement for a book club," she suggested. "But wouldn't the book have a name?"

We drifted through writhing traffic to the beach. "Perhaps a book," I ventured among clashing gears, "which has the sun-gleam of your golden hair in every page, my dear. Or perhaps," and we were tiny trills on the droning monochord of the dark brown sand, "fuck its contents, the book itself has passed through blood and fire, weeping and a tomb, and there's no name for a book like that."

We walked on, and sat where the waves poured in, beneath the crack in the vase.

A golden apoggiatura hushed the grace notes of the wind, sifting the sun-gold strands in an ancient song. And almost, as the comb sang over the strong chord of her breasts, almost, if I peered close, I could make out her face.

"Whether it means," she sang from behind the veil of golden hair, "a book turned inlife out, a hungry book, reading the readers; a wrawling wraxling book, a zoic zoo; a sea-swine falling through faldellas of forget; a vagabundulo, a voice, a void; vardling vastitudes, fatiloquent vambrashing vangles; solivagant on sorrel sands, a songlet unto saintdom." The sun chirped, and the grey waves quavered barcaroles on hidden harps.

Hand in hand, we sang among the shells, walking into the waves.

"Or whether it means, as Wally saw one day, foozling and frisking in the sun's staccato fire in the spring, that the sea gives nothing back, and sheds no tears, but only takes, and vapulates, and is cold..." Her face was stiff and still.

The waves foamed over us like paramours, clasping us eagerly everywhere in the last and closest of embraces. Lightly I loosed her bodice string, laid bare her wave-cold breasts. She, like a blind thing rummaging tentacles for a sea-root in black depths, reached among swaying reeds and pulled it, swollen and dripping like the swollen waves, from my pants. Oh slowly did the soggy sea surrender us back into supernal air. Now green-gold on her head and sea-witch shoulders, eyes foaming greenandgrey, she held me fast, oh unchanging grey changer, and sang farewell, and sucked me off into her icy mouth. And the sapid sea squirmed saltatorily, through me as a universe seething, through all nerves as dying stars in terrible burning, through all long sea-limbs sucked slow and thick as rivers of metals, hungering for the spinal pole, white hot infinities of sea-slime multitudes and spouting in joy sleek salvoes at last of whales swarmed mouthfuls of coronations in white worlds gulped dying through that mask of sun-shot hair. She wriggled with watery cries and was gone under wave-top, into the sacerdotal sable of the deep.

(*Night is falling and the secrets of her face are softer and sweeter now — if I lean close, if I cock an ear shrewdly — yes yes, I can almost hear her voice — whispering goodbye among wave calls...*)

The waves glowed snickeringly and softly with their disgusting secrets now — through black valleys and forests of sea fern I swam to his door and in — the golden walls had changed, were hardly a room anymore, but cavernous and rough, with rocky curves — the desk and chair glowed like an empty throne in a nation without a king.

"Quintus!" I shouted. "Quintus!" My voice bubbling and raging. I pulled out the golden drawers and went through them, letting things fall where they might.

Suddenly he appeared from beneath the desk, smaller than I remembered, and quicker. He was half changed over, scaly and flashing, his beard like sea-weed beneath round flat eyes as he darted about with quick flips of his tail. He scooted along the rock wall soundlessly, nibbling at the sea-weed. "Quintus," I cried, "who from the black caverns of the sea is taking her from me?" And he bubbled at me as if remembering something of my kind of life, and seemed to try to activate something in his throat that wasn't there anymore. "Quintus," I intoned with all the solemnity of my heart, "if the creatures of the sea don't leave her alone I will find you in the deepest ocean cave, and I will crumple you and throw you into the wastebasket and use you to stem the slime beneath my sink, and you will be shut out of the book forever and forever in a void of blank pages where you will have no words to breathe, I —"

But he was gone, old shoulders brushing out the door.

I turn on the cot, listening to the dripping of the sink.

We lie still and watch those stiff grey birds that move with ritual eternality through the fields of blossoms, staidly lifting their graceful feet as they pass under table and chair, by the bed and to the dresser, through the pure leaning stalks. Then we turn toward each other in a trancelike raptness. Each time it is a great, an unlooked-for happiness to recognize each other, and we smile, kiss, cling, and fall away like waves. We gaze at each other through deep water, and it is out in the open between us now, that she has already said goodbye.

(*Goodbye, goodbye.*)

And there are sounds that I cannot place, then the lovely insolent laughter of the bedsprings, and the boat is sailing, the cool waters, the dizzy winds, the new lands

So say it please tremolo
And don't be witty

and it is the land we wanted to wake up and be in, to lie down and sleep in, where the swirling of the tides is dark and deep and pure, and in the jungle of the happy heart the slow beasts swing, and a cold song of farewell, rapt from the leaves of trees that do not die, falls through them like a dream of summer rain

the land where marascas grow

and we sleep.

It's oh so pretty.

Little swamp animals creep close on furry feet and beg gifts of wine-soaked bits from my boat. In time they too are addicted to the mango wine, run to me where I lie drunk on the deck, and gibber in my face, their tiny eyes gleaming. We lie drugged on the moonlit deck and float inward among stairways of color, seeking that central pole, most distant and radiant and never seen, like the heart of a diamond.

19

"My dearest, I will try to tell you now. Quintus is trapped in a book and so am I. And they are all the same."

(*Late sunlight, bubbled by leaf-whorls, dapples my desk and my hands. I think of lies from long ago...*)

"They drip hidden poisons from white petals. They put us in love with what does not exist.

"If we stay at home we are discontented every minute, despise what we once desired, and find at last with helpless rage that long ago we have abandoned life, when first those petals opened.

"Wandering far we grow stupid and do not know it — as a final disgrace come to cherish the memories of old loves which, if we had them still, we would despise...

"At last the foot grows slow, the hand frightened, the eyes dull. We settle down as clerks in small town clothing stores and make no friends. Our new neighbors rightly consider us crazy. We have a fool's dream that someday we will go home.

"Oh dearest, do not think — I fight it, is it true — that I grow sentimental already. Love we all, I think, have tried sincerely and it failed us.

"Listen! What were they that we left behind, the loves? Tinkling things, soft pains thereafter, sweet winces...

"Apples thrown to the ambling feet of a girl, her stunned smiling eyes..."

(*First motes of darkness are moaning around the leaves, which writhe in discomfort.*)

"Say, little gardens that never grew right, which the dogstar parched, earth strangled, or cold rains drowned, just when we had hopes.

"So after the long winter's sleep of darkness and abstention, in the false spring some few spots bloom again, the perennials..."

(*Quintus is dancing his evening dance in the air around me now, and I brush him away but the darkness is falling like tears upon the leaves.*)

"We lie down in relief and joy — the garden is saved! — and for a while delight in the shrubs of love, feel safe and godlike. Then shadows, warnings of thunder...

"We stiffen with cold, burn and scream with lightning, curl up and lie with eyes shut through a barren time, refusing to admit we are alive."

(*A dance of youth that becomes a dance of sorrow — wordlessly he shuffles in the gold suspension, and I see that he has no other way to tell me.*)

"Then the sun, and out of the comforting void — look — it is morning. We stir and roll over."

(*The darkness is covering the leaves and their little screams are strangled and fainter now.*)

"The garden lies desolate. It wants our eyes to pity it. It wants our hands to work it. It wants our lives.

"But under the bushes by the roadway the pages of a book are rustling. Come away, they say, the road, on the other side, lies open and free."

(*Night is here and the leaves are weeping and faded into darkness now.*)

"And yes they are poison, yes yes they are all untrue, but we rise on unsteady legs. We are in love with a dream of life."

(*I go to the window and watch the stars as they whirl on in their perfect dream forever. I am weakened by love for them.*)

"There are other gardens, we say, if we want them. But we think that we will not."

(I turn on the light and electric particles bounce off my giant greyness.

Life is no realer than the laughing of the waves, filled dimly with the passion of a shaft of light.

I go to the sink and pull the plug and watch.

I see the scream her beauty could not utter.

The light is getting finer now. It is falling down around me like rain.

I lie on the cot and seek a clear place among the images.)

> A dream, it is a dream that runs the skies!
> In the darkened field of night some dreamer lies!

One night I woke from a dream in which Quintus was calling me, beckoning urgently. Sitting up in the dark, with Della's breathing and her warmth beside me, I knew at once what the mysterious message was. It was an instalment of the translation I had requested long ago; it was a piece of Quintus's book.

I padded to the table, turned on the light, and read it over and over in the stifling late summer heat. A tingling fear spread through my body.

In the following days others came — records of dynastic successions, genealogies and marriages, burials and reburials. I read them with a confused fascination in the night, putting them together this way and that.

Some search, it seemed, had led Quintus from Smyrna to Egypt, where he visited stonecutters, temples, tombs, questioning aged priests and blowing the dust from ancient books.

There were scraps of songs, lists of names, here and there the edges of a story. . . I read them while the dark angel rushed over. . .

"Radedef he wed Hetep'heres his sister, he wed Khentenka his sister, he wed Meresankh his sister.

"Radedef he killed Ka Wa'ab; Ka Wa'ab his bones lived in Ibn Roash.

"Ank'haf he avenged Ka Wa'ab, he married Meresankh to Chephren the Gizaite.

"Ank'haf sate on the throne that might have gone to the children of Khentenka. And when she bore him a child he named it for the hated daughter, thus filling the place of her through whom royal blood would flow in the sewers of beggary, as if she had never existed."

Winds from the ocean puffed in and Della twitched in her trance of gold. I laid down the papers and went to the window, fear making an emptiness in my heart. I could almost feel in the alleys, where the dogs sat by the cans, someone's feet hurrying in pausing irregular chase, eyes shining, nose snuffling, a hunter.

The next day I went to the library and looked up "Suphis" in a dictionary of antiquities. There was a quotation from someone called Manetho. It said:

> Suphis had a contempt for the gods, and he wrote the sacred book which I acquired in Egypt as being of great value.

Grimly I read on.

> He reared the greatest pyramid, which Herodotus says was made by Cheops.

A librarian guided me to Herodotus on Cheops:

> The wickedness of this man reached to such a pitch that when he had spent all his treasure and wanted more he sent his daughter to the brothel to procure him a certain sum. She procured it, and at the same time, wishing to leave a monument to her memory, required each man who had intercourse with her to make a present of a stone. With these stones she built the pyramid which stands midmost of the three that are before the great pyramid, and which measures along each side one hundred and fifty feet.

Nervously I shelved the fragments of Quintus's book between the *Smyrnaid* and the *Arimaspea*. What did the old creep mean sending me shit like that?

As I left the library the fever of dying summer was dripping down the sides of the buildings. Already the days were getting shorter. It was as if the teeth were springing shut on some trap... But for whom?

I felt the black cloth floating down around us, the bright needles clattering out.

I broke into a run.

20

Come hum the tune at least, my friend,
A song can give them back to us
Old time is gone but new will mend
Come sing, come sing, it's little cost
Be glad you cannot see the end
The torn brain and the pancreas
Oh hum the tune, it's late, my friend,
A song gives back what we have lost

All my lives please me really. It is nice to have always more, always more lives. And easy too. You just walk up, pulling aside the branches of little trees they hang behind, and pluck one off. It's yours...

My raft hangs still on the golden water. Around me time has abandoned its dream of continuity, casting off worlds as it returns through the prism, easy as the swinging of the vines. Music hangs like liquid fire in the air...

The problem is that for each new life you must take a new death too. And that you cannot choose. That you do not know beforehand.
But, oh well.
One day the walk is over. You lie like a spilled cup on the path. Or the game. And you roll down among the bloodied sands...

My step is heavy in the late afternoon as I walk from window to desk. The seasons are burning in their cauldron of gold. Time breaks to a molten flow, like a fountainburst... I think of Della...

The bear just walks up, pushing aside the branches of little trees you hide behind, and takes you down... Or the dancer, rising from the toppling tide with unhurried, even languorous, rhythm, when he (she?) thinks — perhaps for no good reason — that it is time, leaps in a jester's suit to the door, beckons with mask over face, and claims the next dance with you. Shamefaced, or sheepish, you go out...

The songs are not even hushed for other people. In the great sun hall there is hardly a pause in the dancing. They swirl on, over the echoing floor, down the long sand path to the beach, their cuffs, their lacy hems, stained as they trip and twirl, by the brackish blue, by the waiting waves...

When I got back she was lying still, not moving or speaking, her eyes open in the greyness, the works beside her on the bed.

Something foamed over me like the inside of a shell. Something flowed like greasy ashes down my body, some claim grey and cold and old...

My fingers crawled over her face, feeling for the breath, the flutter of the eyelids, the pulse in the temple.

Do not die, my darling, do not die from the filthy disease of living...

Do not stop, till the music is over.

The forest dissolves into a swamp and flows out to the edges of the world, mixing in fire and ashes the volcanic debris of dead oceans. I see myself there, and her —

On the shores of the far seas they stand, awkward unweaned vaguely lovely beasts who do not know where home is, rapt eyes revealing the inner confusion of dimmed wits, pale bodies tinted with briefest fire from a distant sun, soft feet that do not fit in forest, plain, or sea, shuffling in unfelt dance upon the sand, awaiting with inirritable longanimity the stanchless ravishment of the deep.

Della, why did you let them bend you like a stalk of wheat, lonely, and careless what hands harvest it? Didn't you know, didn't you know, that I could take you away to a place where delirium, grown tame, would sing in a cage, and disquietude, demure, would eat from our hands and sleep?

She breathes softly in the darkness.

Time is dissolving freely now, boiling in the oceans of light. Years and timeless years flow through my veins. Memories of ancient universes wash up in the red tides of my heart. Starlit centuries ripple in my breath, like a stand of golden wheat swept by wind...

I lie down beside her in the hungry and primeval dark.

Della once was bright and fair
I kissed her eyes and kissed her where
The darkness she felt growing
Its little seed was sowing

So, Della, you are a cloud now,

    a gentle cow among
    the cattle of the sun

              mooing softly over the blue seas and spilling into the stained green hills like pale milk, a summer rain...
How do you get back together again, Della? And isn't it fun?

    Yes, that must be fun,
    Drifting lightly on...

So the earth is a bad little garden, turning forever and ever in desire for rest,

    which the sun, that ample man,
    tends to when he can
    but when he can't he isn't too distressed.

No rest, no rest, and the bleared stars like bloodied sands...
I breathe deeply in almost sleep and hear them gnawing behind each breath, gasping for rest.

She stirred an eyelid, seeing the veil still over her, and I knew she would come back this time.

"It was..."

"I know," I said.

"It..."

"I know," I said.

A sound.

"I know," I said.

It was Wally. His slimy sea-track was still wet on the floor.

So then you went on a journey, Della, a long way off, fell into the stern of a ship, were mutilated by expert hands (your own), passed the shore where my little bungalow stood by the night-bound jetty, and found the true night, sailing into the great river of the sky. The prow rises, mast leans, and your ship sails into the big void where it is usually dark, past that passionless gardener the sun, and into the weed-strewn field of the universe, flapping your clumsy moth wings and crying sweetly, seeking your home in the unknown zodiacs...

(Fly up, O book)

You fly free in the pure constellations of my fading brain...

21

My girl's eyes are blank and blind
I kiss her front and her behind
Upon her little breast
Lay me down to rest

I rise with a yellow laugh and sing at the window. Malevolent damned book! Then at the sink make morning obeisance to water. Clinging pestiferous book! The day grows full, and I feel it flaring, diffracting, and breaking around me. Then night comes on.

Della would never come back, but I did not believe it. I fitted the needle to the hypodermic and watched the blood leap into its happy world inside. I revisited all the dizzying memories of our lives. I listened to the songs that the wrynecks sang on their harp of wind outside the window. I watched her face (which I have never seen), her breath (which gave the tune to mine), her stillness (which verged now on finality). She turned to me often, her lips seeking mine in sleep. She had entered the first gate, and lay stripped of her golden crown.

Days passed, and summer was winking his eye of gold. We lay still in a reflected abyss, locked in the glass where there was no room to turn. The sun entered an infernal cave, dragging us with it.

While she slept, or while she lay stoned on the bed, I stirred around the little room, looking for signs of her life before I had found her there. In a drawer of the dresser there were dozens of letters never mailed; some had been crumpled then later smoothed for the envelope. In the late nights I read them along with the fragments of Quintus's book.

The waves of the sea piled high, rushing over us. We were fading in the final torments of the sun's ordeal.

"Dear World,
   My name is Della and I need a job. I have no experience whatever in any field of employment and so am equally well qualified for any occupation you may recommend. I am seventeen years old.
                              Love, Della
P.S. I also am in love with a boy named Wally. He never comes to see me though or even writes and what do you think of that. For all I know he's dead or in the navy."

"Fool, do you not see what smoking ruin woman madness wrought for Troy. There is nothing so unmans a man as woman's beauty, it maketh the wise to be fools — but the toil of war. . .ah there is renown."

"I love you so much so softly Wally please love me that is all I want just let me keep your large eyes because I have swallowed the shadow of the soul of you"

Treetops bend at the window. The bus roars on. It is night, morning, night. Rain splashes on the glass.

"Ah fool to board the dusky ship — cries ringing loud in port of Smyrna at night — winds of spring that sort the tresses of youth — but in our hearts was dauntless spirit. . . Call it a dream of the old. . ."

"Girls in general are unforgiveably happy I hate them their games and secrets and terrifying lies which they carry on with stupid glee and play on their coltish long legs with ribboned hair and I feel like shit as usual I love you Wally oh Wally better maybe the way I love you than she they does ever will"

"I will not tell of the lamentation that rose from the deep, I will not tell of the goddesses that wept on the waves, the shining girls, their war-rage maddened faces"

At last I see a far light leaping and creeping through the branches like a thief and the darkness cannot stand against it, the darkness is starting to come apart between its fingers.

"Jesus Wally I wish we were so tiny to live on velvet pansies with striped bumble buzzers for friends and an air blue globe with a heaven I could touch from the inlife side and not be afraid Wally oh Wally my golden earrings are gone and I don't know where I am."

"Tell it ye queens of song... The gods have made her a marvel of beauty even in death. Pain thrills my heart, like eyelids contracting..."

It is dawn and she pulses beneath a web of light upon the cot. She does not move, but soon she will rise and the web will flow down her skin like rain.

"I play with your light hair and wait seconds for O large blue eyes to say nothing being yours and now mine which is everything how long I wonder could we lie talklessly with tiny touches transfixed"

"Fierce lady, dark blood rushed hip to hip — strides into the floes of men — is lapped about by the flaming bronze"

I remember Della from long ago, a child again... The woods we walk through turning green to gold...
"Look, Della! Autumn's coming!"
Della walks through the forest, tiny and faraway.

The old king sits in the late afternoon, bent in the shadows, listening...

"I can't wait anymore Wally Christ I love you but letters can't scream and hold it's funny I sometimes like to think you love me too and that I will be so good to you but I lie groin struck with lightning and your eyes clatter on my bed someday baby you'll love someone as much as I love you and I'll smile to see you writhe impaled on words that no one has ever will say Well just meaning you don't know how much I love you Wally"

"The hills of Smyrna are sweet with snow like the wings of bees. Sea surface thrills with pain. Eyelids contract."

Darkness is devouring the sun, deep darkness, and the day cannot stand against it. Sombrous and lurid it waits for the beamy pale of the lights, their ineffectual fires twinkling down at cockshut time.
The rolling umbrage hungers for eclipse.

"Now sable-vestured night comes floating o'er the wide firmaments of earth, boon of sleep bestowing on sad mortals"

"It's night now and jesus Wally why should I care my body is threaded with starlight sparkled pain jesus Wally I miss you want to see you kiss you you with the writhing brain snake shocking in so mild a child just a trace stuck out here and there with a frenzy which my white breasts may soothe to placidity shit I love you it's no fun anymore it hurts to love this much christ Wally"

Snow falls in the courtyard. Shutters fly open, spilling gold flakes among white. Streaked with tears, a woman's face looks out.

"A dark bride, shadowy and innocent, unfathered in old time . . .old wizard rags of names fall through her hair"

"All mixed up inside this young body are the thoughts of an eighty year old woman very pale and wrinkled like a terrified little animal being stalked"

Worlds rise in floating miniatures above me and drift away upon the breezes.

"Her arms are dark with mummy wings and loud with cries"

Through the window I watch her dance in the twelve gems of her zones.

"I love you as myself with all my heart and all my soul and all my mind and all my strength because I love you so I won't let you die to death I won't honor bright babee"

"Man devourers, Enyo Erinys Eris — Husminai Gorgones and the unhoneyable Fates... Peacocking sea! Dark blood spurts hip to hip."

"Hi babee I love you so much and am so sad that you are gone taking your preposterous belly and wart-nosed back I've kissed the card the envelope the letter the note the name why can't I mail any of them"

The shadow of the turning blades flicks through the light. I sleep and wake and from a passing breeze in the dark I hear Della laughing...
The stars whirl on in their perfect dream forever.

"No sun-god thanks to you you bastard fucker. Obrimothumos... I a brave man why should I consort with the dishonorable"

I awake with a start and find that I am seated at the desk. I feel filthy with nervous guilt. Tears of fear burn in my eyes.
I dip my hands in the greasy water in the sink, then dilute it, retching. The pipes are beginning to sound empty.

"An eighty year old woman so peaceful and thankful for everything but still wanting the joys of youth"

Am I playing the song, or is there someone else who slyly plucks the strings when I am not looking?

"We advance, my flock, to where Melanthus lolls by Hermus stream and will essay the double fortress of his beauty"

They have bad hearts in them, books, weak disloyal hearts.
The skies cannot make them free. The bleared stars cannot contain them.
From their pages, as from the watery abyss, there creeps the nameless and hideous tendency which is lower than the savage beast. On our hearts it leaves its insect trail of bestial cunning.
I sit at the table cluttered with papers all confused.

"I'm not sure Wally maybe it's just as well you're not coming here I don't have anything now and it's kind of fun I guess this is your idea of breaking it off and I guess there's no reason for a reason I love you and I hope I never see you again If there is a heaven I hope you go there and they have warm snow in spring and you odious ORDURE BASTARD I HATE YOU"

Della runs up and splatters me with water, laughs, throwing back her head, and wet-dark strands fall gold-hot prophesying snakes down back and shoulders.
She smiles as when we were children.

"Actually he is merelymine and a golden boy blue and we together are pressed between the yellowed leaves It's near sin how happy you make me I love you I love you"

I am trying to reach you, my dearest, from behind this little pen, these tiny scratches.

"We were lying on the bed in your old house and you did not move and I knew it was not sleep and screamed Wally Wally over so many times but you didn't hear for death I turned on the light but you were laughing and I broke a water glass and killed you with it."

> (*My girl's eyes are blank and blind*
> *I kissed her front and her behind*
> *And kissed the little seed*
> *Of darkness and stampede*)

I regret writing the letters. I regret writing the songs. I regret every word of imagination drawn up from the black deep wheezing with the parasite of memory.
 The lady's veil left fluttering on the shore.
 Its dark devotees.

"I wish I could gather the world into my hands and hear it weep and whisper to its heart-drum how much I love it and after I had held it for ages and timeless time I would spank its round fanny and we would fall awake into the dogbark sparkled dawn"

I empty the wastebasket — the letters the songs the lies — and crouch in the spreading pool of organic slime. Her body looms huge on the cot, a bag of breath filling and emptying.
 There is no sound but the dripping of the sink.
 Why do all books have to end sadly?

"Now I pretend you were my baby and that I stood close to your every side and nothing oh nothing could make you afraid or hurt you and when you are big and have gone too far and are hurt you will come back to my soft white breasts and speak to my quietness and the convulsion of you will shudder and stop on the page of no words"

"It maketh me to sing and not to sing. It maketh me to pour life in this ancient cup."

"I want to be close to you for a rosary of hours"

I wanted this to be a happy book, a gallant flippant book. But I can see it happening here now too. . .

"I want to wear your arms around my neck. I want my clothing and my crown of you"

. . .the people going bad, the minds becoming confused. . . The page howls with crawling, the daylight is smeared with blood.

"Please be close to me please love me closely or send me at least a medal that says Wally in the eardrums of my morsel heart"

You'd better not read any more now, you'd better throw this book away now — something groans shut and they are freeing the clasps from her ankles and from her wrists now — it's the seventh gate

"I will never love anyone as much as I love you and remember when someone calls you a golden boy that you were best when you were my golden boy blue and don't believe her when she says otherwise because she they will never love you hate you as I do"

(Her eyes, will they tell no lies?
Her hair, how the loops ensnare
Her hips oh her icy lips
The mad touch of her fingertips)

"I have come from the hills of Croesus seeking, the hills the ever-virgin walks not weeping"

She is rustling in the darkness, like a net rustling toward me, or a web. She is saying something and I can't understand it. I crouch by the sink in the slime.
"What?" I say.
Something.
"What?"
And she is crawling to the edge of the cot, she is reaching for me, I stare from the slime.
"What?" I say.

Sea slashes with pain.
Eyelids contract.
"What?" and there is singing and it seems not to come from her strained white lips but she is mouthing it.

>*"Oh come with me*
>*Don't you see"*

Her nose, and her mouth, something pours —

>*"I'm waiting*
>*For you"*

Gold, there is gold, and it is flowing —

>*"Anxiously"*

I rush to the bed and she clutches at me, babbling of the injection. Her breasts are burning and the gold flows freely now prodigally and I am afraid to give it to her she is so weak, then there is a scream from outside as her face tears into a greater darkness, a fierce scream as the sea rushes over the charred corpse of summer and the sun burns dying caught at last

>*"Oh come with me*
>*The barren sea"*

She is begging for it and the gold is coming out now nose ears mouth and I want to give it to her I want to it is all I have left to give her I can't tell which of us is dying

>*"Is waiting*
>*For you"*

Her mouth descends in a swirl of blackness onto mine.

>*"Hungrily."*

And we get the injection.

I want to see you I love you I love you christ Wally I try like hell not to think about you I wish it were years from now and we could live together if you wanted but never in one place never never for long I mean I want to see you I miss you I love you it is stupid to love you so much You are not tearing me apart are not are not I hate you I'll never christ I love you Wally christ Wally you've never loved me fine never has perfect ideal strange words first love virginity taken not forgotten given strange horrible first love they smile and the flaming happiness sword of their eyes will blind us now We knew but we tried not to know She weeps because she knew She knew because she is womb Canyon of wombs do not let me die He is the apple of her eye Fallen eaten never known I love Wally I am the source of the canyon of wombs He is my child for the world to admire do not let me die Search for child do not let me die I love Wally I love him
I love love
be kind I love you so

    They are dying at last in my book, I can feel them dying dying. I get up and fall against the desk, then fall against the sink. I pull the plug and fall to my knees and watch it.
    At first it disgusts me that they are dying at last in my book, then it fascinates me. What made their lives dance down the drain like that slurry of scum in my sink?
    Peering close, in fact, I can see them there, their tormented bodies among the bits of trash, waving goodbye.
    Goodbye, goodbye.
    They feel greasy on my hands and I see it then deny it then see it again and turn away. I wipe them in my hair and *what have I gotten into now.* I whisper, *what have I gotten into now.* With difficulty I force myself to look — there is an envelope thrust halfway under my door.
    Goodbye.

    (But we must all agree, you see,
    Della and Wally and you and me)

I stand at the window, among the rag ends of dreams cast into the abyss, and watch the moon set, drifting like a little song into the trees.

Goodbye, goodbye.

22

Oh when the moon sails out
Astrologer, astrologer
Then will be lookout knockout blackout
Then will be shutout getout without
Oh when the moon sails out
Astrologer
Then will be breakup ripup hiccup
Then will be situp gitup giveup
Oh when the moon sails out
Astrologer

I stagger up, weightless and dull, and don't know where I am. *Morning,* the light says, edging in the window. My foot kicks something and it is a hypodermic. *Morning, and there is much that we must do.* It skitters under the bed.

There is an unread letter on the table and taking it from the thin blue envelope I lean over it, head in hands.

"I'm writing you letters again that I don't send and so I took up giggling but that was no remedy."

Della is lying on the bed in stopped gold, her hair in her eyes and mouth, the bedsheets twisted thickly around her thighs.

Morning, the grey fish says, bumping his nose at the window.

> Get up there! Don't you see
> They're calling you and me
> The time for secret darknesses is gone

The grey fish is swimming over to her now.

It must be from Cracow, I think, it must be my reply from Cracow, Cracow. Almost stealthily I lean and snatch it up, my fingers dangerously near the crack under the door. Strangely, I find that it bestows a warm feeling on my arm. It occurs to me for no reason that it is an invitation to a party. Tears of happiness press at my eyes. It makes me feel that you are here, my beloved, raising your hand to strip off the final veil. I turn quickly, looking around the room. I can feel you coming closer, within the air, within the light, rustling near...

"Merely a hemoglobin deficiency, the doctor said, but then something must be in excess and I don't know what."

Della, I say, turning toward her, was it the gold, Della, was the gold in excess, Della? I look at her dully where she will not rise in gold.

"Children tricycling over the merrymeads, unconscious of age which eats its dessert first."

I hold it over the desk, turning it in my hands, and it feels familiar, it feels like — Dizziness comes over me, like the inside of a shell. I can almost remember leaning toward that crack in the vase, thrusting something through it with a sudden impulse, to see if anyone would notice...

With shaking hands I pick up a page from my book and — the writing is the same.

The room is getting lighter with that watery greyness which is not yet stained with any gold, which has no name but is an insult to us all.

        Get up, you slugabed!
        We all wish we were dead
        But morning clasps cold hands around the house

"Della," I cry, and my voice is hard to recognize. "Della, get up!"

The sun is beginning to swim through the greyness in a milky stain now.

"Della!" and my voice is a roaring bark that fills the aquarium.
The sun clatters like a dropped flashlight on the sill. Gold flops like a stunned bird through the window. The day rises in fire and leaps upon her bed. I cannot move.

> That burning yellow ape
> Has got a bent for rape
> So cover yourself up and look alive

"Della," I am barking over and over so many times. And I wallow to the bed and take her in my flippers and hold her all the burning day, shielding her from the loathesome fires that hurt.

> (*I kissed her eyes and kissed her where*
> *The darkness she felt growing*
> *Its little seed was sowing*)

And at first it seemed less sinister that I had written it myself, but at second thought more. And finally it didn't seem to matter.
For no reason at all it occured to me that even the planets were dying, that their dream too was coming to an end, the constellations with their insect trails across the sky, the alien zodiacs fading in the midmost silence of my heart...
I tore it open, breathing loudly, and caught the little paper which fell out almost too fast, almost eagerly, recognizing as if from centuries past the familiar thaumatropic script —

> *Come out with me*
> *The barren sea*
> *Is waiting*
> *For you*
> *Anxiously*

It was my invitation to the party.

But there was no RSVP.

23

(I have kept you from his grip
His fires can't hurt you now
Yet still touch lip to lip
Brow to loving brow

    be kind I love you so   be kind I love you so
Della oh Della   Della

My girl's gold no longer flows
Blood not breath comes out her nose
Now she has no chance
To do her weeping dance

Della oh Della I have kept you from his grip, his fires can't hurt you now, the flames can't get you now, the sun that kills, that careless gardener who crushes down the plants who burns them down, and when we bring him blossoms he devoureth them

Look darling he has changed and we shall too
The moon has changed and now we shall be new

now it is dark and when the moon sails ohh when the moon sails
Della out of your eyes and the moon will tumble the dark of the light,
the pale dead gold of the night ohh when the moon sails Della

> *Out of your eyes when the moon sails Della*
> *Out of your eyes and the night*
> *Will tumble the floodlight skylight twilight*
> *Goodnight Della goodnight*
> *Will tumble the redlight stoplight termite*
> *Goodnight Della goodnight*

Goodnight

be kind I love you so

goodnight goodnight)

24

A sob escapes me, loud, and full of despair. I paw at my papers, tear them, groaning, shred and throw them. They float like a broken face about my room.

"I loved Della truly," I say, my voice a disgusting whine that sickens me even as I hear it, but I do not stop. "I loved her truly, and now, O book, O suffering pestilential book, you tell me what to do."

(Come sing, come sing, it's little cost)

Suddenly I hear the roar of the engines — the bus is racing — a strange crippled motion — the aisle is filled with people — someone has pulled the bell-cord and someone else is shouting goodbye and someone else is weeping — packages are being pulled from shelves, scarves tied around necks — the driver's seat, beneath the rain-spattered windshield, is empty. Figures bump in the shadows and are gone. A girl's voice keens under the desert moon. The tresses of her hair fly out in a dreamy dance. . .

Going to my window I gaze for hours at the stars. The pitchy caligation gobbles up their nitid flares? Ah no. These lordings march aright, these dynasts of the night, they only want a chance to tell their story.

> *Do you dream, little stars,*
> *Venus, do you dream of Mars,*
> *Of a grand and good conjunction*
> *Full of lovers' benediction?*

Where are you, my dearest? I rub my eyes. Where is it, my dearest?
 I feel for the light switch and clickclickclickclick.
 My light has gone out!
 The lamp has gone out!
 Someone has pulled the plug outside my room!
 I can feel the brazen door begin to swing slowly open.

> *Do you dream, silver moon,*
> *That your dance is ending soon*

I turn wildly, staring into the darkness as if it might show me something.

> *Your shining partner's hot embrace*
> *Loosening to silver peace?*

At once I realize that I shouldn't have turned because now I don't know where I am in the room. If it was a fuse the fan would have gone off too but I can feel it turning and turning in the darkness sharper than razors faster than winds trying to cut me I think — I hold my breath and it cannot hold its though it wants to — I hear it sniffing the air, riffling through papers on the desk, sending them in a long stream through the dark — swinging its glaring head, trying to find me.
 Quietly now I'll shuffle my feet hurry on old foot I can inch along I can find the desk I can feel it there I can feel for the letter and hold my breath and shuffle my feet to the light of the window if there is light I can see the postmark why did I not look for the postmark if there is a postmark it must be from Cracow if there's a postmark it is Cracow Cracow

Yes you dream, all little stars
Poets' fancies, princes' wars

That gnawing is louder in the walls, and there is a crawling sound with it now too, yes and in the floor, tiny feet, a tiny song of breath

A prevalence of caterpillars
Spilling from your golden collars

and it is a song of youth I hear — the vast army of brute life on the hunt and eager to be born — something has me by the throat —

While you dream you make our lives

a wind of death — enters me and I rise — the fan cord! — the fan — it is on me, cutting — spurting, my hands — embraces me, clings — I crash to the floor as it cuts in for the kill

Jupiter likes Uranus's wives

but I rise in great strength from the pile, tear it off and fling it away among the dunes — wingcrack by swampedge — a broken face —

Saturn climbs into a boat

"If Saturn be Lord of the Year" — yes that must be it — "and if he enter into Taurus" — yes yes — "death to the fish in the rivers" — "a scarcity of water at the fountains" — "thin unhealthy air and dark clouds" — I stagger backward and fall upon the cot, leap up — "If retrograde, let the ruling monarch beware for his life" — "Destruction and violence!" — dreams are breaking up inside like tidal floes —

Hoarse cries issue from his throat

And yes I hear them in the hallway now with their robes of stars and impaling stakes — shuffling their feet and coming toward the door — I drop to all fours — there is still time to think, they can't stop that yet — but wait — if I listen close — there is only one person out there, really — clearing his throat — impatient but still polite — waiting — How dare he clear his throat at me! — yes that must be it — the footman, who brought the invitation, he awaits my reply — I clear my throat — I'll say, No thank you not just now please — I'll say I'm feeling poorly later some other time please — he shuffles his feet — How dare he shuffle his feet at me! — Haven't I told them the palace door will never, will not, will never never open again — belching its fire and thunder its birds and gold — those riches I have locked within now — the sad king alone in the darkened throne room — stung to mad brooding — around me the tunes of dances slithering in the slime — that other world exists no more. An odor rises and I know it well — the grey void under the flower — yes yes I can smell us now — we are in the spilled papers dearest the torn face on the floor — I can smell us being broken down to our smallest elements again — the smell of lives wrung out and done — the shining slime — it clings to my hands — I lick my fingers and it tastes like you, beloved — tears press at my eyes — I taste your little seed, of darkness and stampede...

And yes I understand now, it is you outside my door, pirouetting on your dainty feet, slow and sad with the stars in your hair as you spin...

Neptune blinks his watery eye

I remember, I remember — they are bursting around me in the darkness like bubbles of bright scenes fading forever — I remember pale faces from long ago — the knights in Cracow revolting against the king — yes that is it — I remember now — they come closer — their heels, their robes — astrologer in dark castle — rumors of conspiracy and in the morning a drunken singer seated on the throne — for sceptre the bent horn — for diadem, the reeling stars that glitter in his eyes. I see them clearly now, only I cannot tell which face is mine — or yours.

The door to my room bursts open in bronze and fire — I see a candlelit hall — the fiddles resound on the echoing stones — heedless of the fate of worlds the dancers brush by the door.

Dark figures drag her in. My daughter! My daughter!

O singer of dreams, on your strings of flames, defend her!

After several days I picked her up in my flippers and put her in the trunk of my car. She was happy and smiling. Little clouds danced brightly overhead. We drove out to the sunny bridge, where the seabirds fly.

I called "Della oh Della" to the clouds, and they rained happy gold. I cried "Look oh look" to the waves, and they foamed hungrily. I cried, "Look, waves, I am bringing Della to you, sing to her!" and crashing on the rocks beneath the bridge they sang

> Come to me
> Come to me
> I'm waiting
> For you
> Hungrily

And I gave her to them.

Pluto's wagon rattles by

And I dove high, pockets full of heroin and a razor blade taped behind the buckle of my belt, and I swam deep, churning my flippers fast and eagerly, where the rolling anemone toils.

Kings die still, and days make years

I bump against the sink, stand up, and open the faucets all the way — they are empty. Scarcity of water at the fountains. Sea slashes with pain.

Look, Della, the woods we walk through turning gold to white...

And I know now, my dearest, I know when autumn flares that we will flush like burning leaves, curl, and be dry, and come apart in the hands of the wind...

While you dream, little stars.

There is a scratching in the dark like some little beast requesting entry. It moves along the walls and is fumbling at the door now. I bump against the cot and leap away.

The scratching comes again, but louder. And with a click, then a storm of plucked strings, the door swings open.

And you call for me. It's time for the party, you say, lay down your work now.

And noiselessly, but I can feel it like clicking blades, you come near.

"Do you come from Cracow," I ask, confused, but I am a great fool, and you ignore that.

"I have come for you, old one," you say. "You can come out now."

And I had not realized that the door was locked.

Quickly, like a rush of air, your fingers are tangling in my beard, your hands are reaching within my cloak and coolly, lovingly, gathering me in. Your hair comes down like a swarm of birds, your breath is in mine, I hear the insistent music calling to the party, a flute on a nightship, and we are away, past the menacing blades and the pages that ripple beneath them, out the window and onto the billowing cushion of night.

As I cling to you and we rise up past the dark tips of the elms, I sense an absence, and look back, through the window where the lights are on, and the floor is being swept, and it is autumn.

My desk is empty.

Quickly I look above.

And beyond us, over the waves of the sea, my book flutters up on its dark apalling wings.

And I am gone.

Higher, higher, and I do not know what it means, I do not know how it works, that the wings of the crow shall nourish the sun with brightest flames.

(Be caught by none of them)

25

When I woke up the bus was chugging through the outskirts of some little city and heading into a desert. The sun was sinking low and its late rays raked through the windows. I got off at a little oasis as shadows were spreading over the seats and the heads of sleepy travellers. Outside, the day was hot and stifling. On the left was an oasis pool overhung by a white cypress tree, and on the right a stand of sycamore, willow, and alder. Turning into their cool shade I came to a little spring, where I drank, washed, and leaned over the bright surface, straightening my hair and tie. A little path led to a cottage, with sun-window. As I approached there was a sound of singing, which stopped when I knocked on the rough wood of the door.

In a moment he opened, shading a lidded reptilian face from the setting sun, and beckoned me through a dank little hall where a mangy dog slunk away. In a large room dim with smoke a veiled girl sat by the chimney, the seeds of a blood-red fruit staining her fingers and her veil.

"Sit down," he said. "Like a drink?"

I nodded — "Whatever you're having" — and stared at her in fascination till he came back. Her breath puffed out the veil, labored and slow. In a moment a cold glass was slipped into my hands and I had almost drunk from it when I realized what a perfect damned fool I was and lowered it hastily, spilling some on my shirt.

I felt there was no need to apologize. "Give me yours," I said.

He smiled with a hint of mockery in his eyes and we exchanged glasses and settled back in facing chairs before the hearth. I watched him sip from mine and, thinking uneasily that he must have known I would ask to exchange them, tried to remember if he had drunk yet from the one I was holding. There was amusement flickering on the surface of his face as he watched me, but something else, something that did not feel right, something that would never feel right, lying like a bare blade underneath.

"Would you like yours back?" he asked with exaggerated, even sarcastic, courtliness. I shrugged, aware of playing the fool, and toasted him, as the host, then drank.

"It's like the flowers," you know, I said, and he made a gesture as if to say *of course,* or *I understand,* and said nothing. "Did you plan the order I would take them in?" I asked curiously.

"Of course," he said at once. "I had heard enough about you from Quintus to know you would recognize the red one and take it immediately. That was to lead you on. Then the not-quite-blue," he went on with wrinkled brow, "was to have brought you —" he motioned to the girl slouched by the crumbling hearth, the flowery robe twisted thickly around the mounds of her thighs, and said, "to her."

"Well," I said, prevaricating slightly, "so it did. As you can see."

He seemed not to care, and turned aside his gaze. "Too late," he said softly.

We sat still for a while and calls of birds came from outside, like splinters of metal falling icily in the smoky firelight. She stirred, with a rustling of silk, and they stopped.

I was silent for a moment deciding what to ask him first. "So tell me," I said, "what happened to Quintus."

Again he made a gesture as of nothing, as of something that didn't matter, and said, "Dead. Oh yes. Died happy though, if you care about that."

"Yes," I murmured. I remembered his slobbering dances under the river, his insane apparitions in my dreams. "How did he die?"

"She killed him," he said, motioning.

I looked from him to her and back. "I read his book, of course," I said. "And I could put two and two together. As he had. A little work in the library...

"He had found in old books, in scraps of the histories that are now lost, the story of the princess, Suphis's daughter supposedly, whose mother was half-Libyan, and how the genealogies skip a step there because someone long ago wanted something left out... The cemetery moved from Ibn Roash for no reason, the bones of the elders moaning over the desert sands... How the girl's mother had taken as lover some criminal, some beggar or wandering minstrel, by whom the daughter was begotten. How they killed the king, and that prince of beggary sat upon his throne..."

He neither nodded nor bared his glittering gaze, and for a moment I was embarrassed to be talking about his private affairs like this.

"For god's sake, I was practically there," I said. "I've had dreams you wouldnt believe...all that creeping down corridors..." I got up and paced back and forth in the room.

"So they moved the cemetery and fixed the records — even if Quintus had found the Suphis book it would probably have been altered. But it wasn't enough. There was still Suphis, her son by the real pharaoh, to deal with."

He stirred impatiently. "Yes yes but it was not her son. The pharaoh's son by another wife. Who was not Libyan." We sipped at our drinks for a minute while the girl sat slumped and still.

"Some god story, probably," I conjectured, "that somehow this was still the king, that he was transfigured into Osiris, looked different...and he stayed out of sight behind masks and barred gates... But they knew how that story ended, too. The problem was to avoid the fight with the son, the Horus fight." His face showed some annoyance. "It's only amazing that he didn't kill them both," I said, watching him. "The woman perhaps he killed. But the man knew all the sewers and alleys and byways that anyone who was not either a magician or a fool would fear to walk in." I looked at the girl and wondered if she was following what we said.

"Here was the catch," I said softly, still gazing at her. "While

[215]

they had lived together as king and queen in their palace garden, they had, of course, a daughter... And her the new pharaoh, Suphis or Cheops or Chephren, kept behind, to strike through her at the beggar man who had escaped."

"No beggar," he said softly. Abruptly he rose and I thought he was going to tell me to leave, but he didn't. "A king," he said with finality. "A great king."

And now it was my turn for amusement and courtesy, so I smiled and said, "But a king who knew songs. A king who knew flowers and poisons... Not a king who knew armies, treasuries, ships..."

He looked at me with contempt and it seemed certain that he would ask me to go at once, but it had been a long time since he had had anyone to talk to about these things.

"And that daughter," I went on, "who was one quarter of the true flesh anyway, the new king — her half brother — adopted as his own, and to debase that branch of the royal line forever he put her to work building with the flesh of her body that pyramid to conquered love. And there are many stones in it..." The room was still but I thought I could hear someone breathing. "Until her real father," I said, "found her in one whorehouse (let's not ask how) and took her into another, to work for him.

"And so if she had children the blood of the palace would run in the beggars of Egypt to this day, a little stream diverted for a royal joke from the river of divinity." He sat stiff and proud.

"And when the others were gone," he said harshly, "killed by the Persians with their impaling stakes, or extinct from incest" — he stopped, and I continued for him — "then those children of gods who were lost in the sewars of beggary, sunk in the teeming slums, were all that was left of the garden of heaven on earth."

I looked at her where she would not rise in gold. "And Quintus figured it out" I murmured, "for he hated the new gods. And he knew that somewhere he might find a girl who was fit by blood and nature to sit on the throne of Egypt, a goddess in the flesh..." And my voice was hushed.

"I heard some old fool was looking for the girl," he said, "for the princess Meresankh as he thought she was no less. There had been others before him," he said contemptuously. "A foreigner. Might have money. So I sent her after him. Got his books when they cleared out his room. The one he reached for first I sent to you. With the flowers. It was only for ransom. Or to catch a bigger fish." He was silent for a moment. "I didn't expect to get another eccentric for my trouble."

He talked on in the dimness — and I thought he would look tired and old now, but he didn't — told of schemes, kidnappings, ransoms, governments, revenges, trying to establish her upon the throne of the world, a mother for all creation. How he had needed money for one more mad intrigue within the palace. How when he had gotten none from Quintus and couldn't either let him go, because he knew the house and everything that went on there, or kill him, because the girl was fond of him, and sensitive, he had suffered with rage the humiliation of feeding that worthless old mouth and hearing it abuse him. How he had used the girl to draw in Christopolous to strike through him at those who ruled with no right. And how when the girl went mad and killed Quintus with love, he used my friend's old body instead in a final joke, then fled beneath the river. "And Christopolous?" I asked, for he had told me of the freedman's falling in love with her. "Oh he got a job in a dry goods store, I think. In Sarepta. Or Dora Dor. Became the local eccentric.

"Would you like another," he said rising, then went to mix more drinks. She sat hunched by the fire, motionless except for the veil floating out with her breath. The great curves of her body were piled high with the dark-flowered garment. I dreamed of the beauty she must have had once, how I and many others had spent our lives seeking it in the snowy fields. . . And when he stepped back into the flickering light, handing me the cold-beaded glass, I said, "So what does she look like now? It's time that I saw her." He nodded, and a quietness came over us.

He went to the hearthside and reached for the veil slowly, as if not to startle her. Still she pulled away sharply and would, I felt, have screamed at him if they had been alone. He coaxed her as one would a sullen child, with some threat in the coaxing too, till she turned her head slowly toward me. Then he pulled aside the veil.

I caught just a glimpse of the nauseating mess disease had made, before she pulled it back. Feeling ill, I only murmured to affirm that I had seen, then looked away from them both. When he sat back down there was not much more for us to say.

"What was it you gave her?" I asked.

His gaze did not break, was glittering and jittering like knives, as he took a drink, then said, "syphilis," and veiled his eyes, "or rather, an older and more virulent form of it." I had the feeling he was smiling but the dust of night was drifting through the air now and I couldn't see, when suddenly he glittered full on me.

"It is a small yellow flower," he said softly.

I gazed at him with considerable heat for quite some time.

"That," he said finally, "was in case you survived the blue one. I couldn't let you get around with what you might know by then..." He made the dismissive gesture again, half polite, half arrogant, and said, "But evidently you have not got to it yet. You look alright, anyway."

"Yes," I said, "so do you."

It was getting darker and he sat, a shadowy king, ancient and savage and evil, on his dismal throne. In the last wisps of light I thought with a dying sadness of Della, who had tasted that yellow flower and it devoured her, and even of Wally, who had crashed down the stairs with it in his gut.

I blinked, and looked at him over the rim of my glass. "Personally," I said, "I deal in injections."

We looked at each other and there was a certain clash, a certain wrestling, in our glances.

We would both have been kings of song. We would both have eaten all flowers. Now our princesses were gone, but we lived on, lonely and indestructible and cruel, like the songs the waves sing on the deep. The room was very still, and darkening quickly now.

"So who are you," I said at last, clearing my throat, "how long have you lived, following that whore of a princess down the generations with your nooses of flowers, your songs from murderous horns?"

He turned the glass around and around in his hands and this time I was sure that he was laughing silently, or smiling, but the dust of night lay thick upon the glass now and I could not see.

"Do not ask who I am," he said softly before the last gleam was gone. And he didn't need to finish.

I could feel my eyes glittering against the veils.

26

When I looked back at Vincent's house, hoping, for no good reason, that she might follow me, the door slammed shut. In front of me the first light of morning was creeping across the desert. I flagged the bus down and jumped on. A ray of sunlight swirled in the empty driver's seat like a little song, and the busride also was like a little song, bursting out in my heart with sweet swellings.

> *Oh come with me*

I sang, touching the smiling passengers on the arms — bachelors and brides and the old who have suffered all — walking down the aisle of polished seats.

> Oh come with me
> The restless sea...

I got off and saw a little cloud floating overhead, crossing a river and hanging over a little green hill.

> "Della, Della!"
>
> I cried, and ran after it. And yes, it was Della. I heard her sweet familiar voice in a little song,

> *Oh come with me*
> *The broken sea...*

Della, Della! I cried, but she was too fast, floated sweetly smiling over and away.

I passed through a little town where people were just waking up, climbed the hill to the castle, walked through the courtyard where snow stilled the steps, and tried the locked door. Getting no answer I followed the endless, changing walls, found a great cliff in back, looking up saw broken windows. Below, the cold sea slobbered patiently.

Breaking a window, I went in and walked through the cold stone rooms.

"Della, Della," I called,

> Come out with me
> The laughing sea
> Is waiting
> For us
> Patiently.

In one of the rooms I found her, huddled beneath the bed, a frightened bird on the grey stone floor. Putting her in a pocket of my beggar's coat, I walked on.

Soon there was a blast of cornets and a dry shaking of old lace in the throne room. I went in and sat on the throne and there was cold regal music from the breaking waves in back, where ice was thrown about the rocks.

Then the others came in, a limping cornet player, a tyrant with songs in his beard, a bear with snow on his back.

"Where is the lady?" I asked.

"Too proud," they said, and I went out, walked through the long halls and echoing chambers till I found her, O dark one, like a little bird lost in a pillowy bed. I put her in the other pocket and went out, through the clashing bronze doors, as the others followed.

We climbed down the cliffs in back and threw pieces of ice into the moaning sea. His feet wrapped in rags, the cornet player shuffled up.

"Are you death," I said, "or am I?"

He smiled with broken teeth and pointed the battered and blood-stained horn at me. I pointed at him, and we laughed.

"Come on," I shouted, and we leapt out onto the ice. The cornet began to squeal and the waves sang and parted and I marched on to the rattle of watery drums and the trilling of sunny clarinets.

Come out with me!

The waves rose up to sleepy fields and by weeping willows and wishing wells librarians lay like sick grass. I strode through their assembly and they wilted back. But we played,

The broken sea!

and they came, and from waveside a dancer leapt up and reeled over with sea-weed streaming head.

"Are you death," I said, "or am I?" He pointed at me and we laughed.

Oh who is death, we sang?
The walrus in the stream!

and from the water a flipper splashed with a barked *hello*.

The throne without a king
The dreamer of the dream

And I marched on and the trumpets blared around.

> The sea the happy sea
> And clouds up in the sky
> And girls who wickedly
> Wink a laughing eye

And they gathered around and we kept right on.

> Oh who is death, we sang
> And what is he to us?
> A ring, a rang, a clang,
> A bright and empty bus

> Oh Della was killed by Wally
> And Wally was killed by me
> So who is death? The jolly
> Old men dance on the sea

I marched on through the palaces and the libraries and the echoing halls,

> And we sang where the sea-shells sing
> In the depths of the laughing blue sea.
> And the others dropped off one by one
> Drifting to the bed of a girl
> Who beckoned and smiled and toyed
> With the lacy strings of the veil.

And there were rooms that burned with fire, and empty hotels where my life lay moaning in dreamed unhappiness, and at last, when there were no more songs to sing, I gave a happy cry, and, opening my pages like dark wings
               fluttered off
                             over the rooftops
                                           of the waking